NO REGRETS, NO SURRENDER

Includes the prequel
Retreat Hell! She Just Got Here

BY

HEATHER LONG

ଓଃ

Decadent Publishing Company
www.decadentpublishing.com

No Regrets, No Surrender
Copyright 2013 by Heather Long
ISBN: 978-1-61333-424-9
Cover design by Mina Carter and Cribley Designs

Published by Decadent Publishing Company
www.decadentpublishing.com

Printed in the United States of America

RETREAT HELL!
SHE JUST GOT HERE

Chapter One

The toe ring felt damned weird. It rubbed, and despite the clucking of the woman painting her toenails, Jazz couldn't stop wiggling.

"Toe rings are sexy, sweetheart. Now sit still." The chiding voice carried a level of amusement that she didn't share.

With a long sigh, Jazz looked away from the *fuck me* red that the woman, Christine might be her name, applied to her toes, and stared in the mirror. Her normally smooth, even hair cut had been replaced by a mussed mass of curls clinging to her cheeks. Eyeliner magnified her eyes and one of the other women had given her *the smoky look*, whatever the hell that meant.

She'd never looked so much like a girl.

Ever.

The opulence of the spa matched the refinement of the rest of the Castillo Resort. The feminine reflection staring back at her made it hard to believe she'd arrived that morning in jeans, an old Kiss band T-shirt and sneakers that she'd bought in high school. The whirlwind packing that led to her early morning flight out of Dallas hadn't left her much time to shop, but everything from the soak in the hot tub, to the hour-long massage, to the hair dresser, personal shopper, makeup artist, and now her nails, all came in the prearranged package.

Her nails.

Stealing a second glance at her toes, she swallowed a laugh. The guys would be hooting if they could see Gunnery Sergeant Winters wiggling long, toes against the plush foot rest. Her legs were waxed smooth along with every other part of her body except her bikini area. When the spa technician suggested it and came at her with wax, Jazz had threatened to put her down like a two-hundred-pound trainee.

She'd earned her sergeant stripes and she wasn't kidding.

"There, all done. Now sit here for a few more minutes, dear, and we'll take you back so you can change." Christine patted her leg in an almost motherly fashion, before rising to clean up her tools. Sinking back in the massage chair, Jazz studied her reflection in the mirror. She was that sexy thing the men loved to swap tales about late under the cover of darkness to disguise the urge to go home. She saw exactly what she'd hoped—a woman. Not a sergeant.

Not a Marine.

Her fingers were painted the same sexy shade of red. A set of acrylic tips camouflaged her squared off and blunt nails. Nothing could hide the calluses on her palms, worn grooves from years of handling weapons and driving. But the nails definitely added a level of feminine grace, making her short stubby fingers tapered and elegant.

"Ready?" Her personal shopper returned, her name might have been Anne, but after the whirlwind of men and women fussing over her throughout the day, it could have been Amy or Annabelle.

"Yes." No. *No, I'm not ready.* She still couldn't believe her mother had taken her late night confession to heart and signed her up with the exclusive 1Night Stand dating service. Even harder to believe that in seven days the mysterious Madame Eve, of the mile long interrogatory questionnaire, identified and arranged the perfect night to meet Jazz's goals.

Jasmine.

With white cotton balls still peeking between each toe and the toe ring flashing silver up at her, she followed the shopper back, and reminded herself that tonight she wasn't Jazz. She wasn't one of the guys. She was Jasmine.

For just one night, she would be a woman, not a Marine. But the woman needed the Marine when she nearly had a heart failure at the almost-not-there dress.

Ω

Zach tipped the bellman who insisted on carrying their two bags up, and retrieved the duffels before shuttling the gregarious and welcoming young man from the room. Zach didn't think, *hoped*, he'd ever been that wet behind the years. Across the room, his best friend and *brother-in-arms*, Logan, stared out at the sun-splashed Strip below. They had an hour until their date would arrive.

The suite at the Castillo Hotel and Resort appeared exactly as described in the brochure: plush. He spared the décor a glance, itemizing the location more on layout than on content. A square, oversized wraparound sofa took up much of the central part of the room. The smooth taupe tapered down to the cream-colored carpet with a splash of color reflected against the southwest style pillows. Beyond that sat a blonde oak dining table and four chairs, lamps, some side tables and a fifty-inch television screen.

Zach's gaze zeroed in on it. Dropping the bags next to the door of the suite's single bedroom, he located the television remote and pressed the on button. They had time to catch the last quarter of the game.

"I'm going to go ahead and order dinner up." He found the room service menu waiting on the table. "Any preferences or should I just order one of everything?"

"What I'd prefer is to head down for some blackjack." Logan's clipped words betrayed neither fatigue nor excitement. "Then you can make like bunnies with your project."

"Survey says, ehhhhh." Kicking his feet up onto the polished table, Zach caught the score. The Cowboys were down by three. But they could still rally. "The date is for both of us and you agreed to it."

"Only because I thought you'd come to your senses. What the hell kind of woman agrees to a blind, one-night stand with two men she's never met?" Logan didn't bother to wait for a response. "The kind who is going to be less than thrilled when she finds out one is a cripple and here for a pity fuck."

Rubbing his right forefinger against his thumb, an old trick that helped him relax his nerves, nerves he didn't have time for right then, Zach twisted to look at the stiff line of Logan's back. He still stared down at the Strip. His brother missed the joke, poor one that it was. "Dude, you agreed. It's both of us or neither of us. Just give it a shot."

"Why?" Logan swung around, revealing the harsh twist on the left side of his face, the corner of his mouth permanently turned in a grimace. Scar tissue puckered from his cheek to his throat would never again allow the easy grin. He'd been more relaxed before his injury—a reminder of the burning, twisted metal coffin that led to five surgeries, three pins, one in his knee, one in his hip and the last one in the shoulder. Months of physical and mental therapy later, Logan walked and talked, but he refused to live.

After weeks in Germany, they'd relocated to Bethesda Naval Hospital until Logan took his first real steps twelve weeks ago. It took some cajoling—and no small amount of bullying on Zach's part—to convince him to accept the offer from the recently opened Mike's Place in Texas. Captain Luke Dexter—Marine and son of Colonel Dexter, Zach and Logan's commanding officer who'd been killed in the same bombing that put Logan in the hospital—wanted to offer them the first berths in his new mental and physical health center.

Zach didn't need the mental or physical therapy, but he

and Logan were a package deal. So, he'd taken a job working with the children's sports teams, coaching the sons and daughters of the service families currently residing on property or using the facilities. Logan benefitted from the therapy and the work.

"Because a deal's a deal and we all signed up when the Captain did." Dexter didn't need the service anymore than Zach did, but they'd been in agreement. Some of the men, like Logan, wouldn't even contemplate looking at another woman. Particularly after his bitch of a girlfriend, Rochelle, made a scene in front of the others, calling Logan's impotence to light.

It didn't help that every doctor called the condition psychosomatic. Logan had convinced himself sex wasn't going to happen. But they'd shared girls before, twice in high school and once on leave in Germany. Logan would've turned down this opportunity solo, so a threesome it would be.

"Whatever. What's the score?" He ended the conversation, his posture closed off and his expression remote. Zach left it alone. He knew fear when he saw it. Fear was a tangible part of the everyday life of a Marine. They'd done their tours overseas, Afghanistan, Kuwait, and Iraq. Their 'soft tour' as diplomatic support landed them front and center in the Egyptian riots. Catching a bullet at any moment was their reality.

Fear didn't stop a Marine.

And it wasn't going to stop Logan tonight.

"Ten-seven, but we've got another quarter to go. They could pull ahead." Zach glanced back down at the menu. "I'll get us some of these appetizer platters, three steaks and maybe one of the fish and veggie dishes. I didn't see anything on her sheet about being a vegetarian."

Logan grunted, pacing the room behind him. The nervous energy pressed against the back of Zach's head, but he did his best to ignore it. Pacing served as a coping mechanism. After the two and a half hour flight, Logan had to be stiff.

Ordering the food, Zach kept one eye on the game. The

fumble gained the Cowboys ten yards, but not enough for a score. He glanced at his watch. The fifteen minutes since they'd arrived seemed a hell of a lot longer. Logan's pacing continued, promising an even longer forty-five minutes until their date got there.

The paperwork described their date, Jasmine, as five-foot eight inches tall; she enjoyed sports, preferred baseball to football and wanted a night of total escape with two partners. The rest of the information focused on the Castillo Resort, their room reservation and the time of the date. It wasn't a hell of a lot to speculate on.

The Cowboys lost the ball, Zach sighed. The Packers seemed intent on flattening his home team. His thoughts returned to their date. She wanted a night with two men. He only hoped that she lured Logan out of his shell or it would all be for nothing.

Forty-five long minutes later, the food waited patiently under silver lids. The staff had rolled in a no-frills table with a simple white cloth covering the portable surface. Zach could damn near taste the steak, but at least Logan wasn't pacing anymore. A pair of light staccato raps on the suite door echoed through the sitting room. Muting the game, Zach headed for the door. He didn't miss the hard tension stiffening Logan's posture.

Not letting himself dwell on the dozen ways this could go wrong, he opened the door to the sexiest pair of legs he'd ever seen. Zach's entire body went taut, his cock thrumming into an erection between one heartbeat and the next. The long tan legs were attached to a pair of flared hips. Flat tummy, curvy waist and higher still to the firm, full breasts threatening to spill out of the plunging V neckline that ended at her belly button. Her skin was a rich golden sheen, kissed by the sun, but not quite tanned.

A winsome face, smoky black eyes and a pixie cap of curls completed the package. If not for the silk sheathe, she looked like she'd just tumbled out of bed.

Fuck me...please....

The thought echoed through his brain, locking his tongue.

"Mr. Evans?" The woman's—Jasmine's—brows lifted, her sexy mouth tilted up into a half smile, the patient kind women used when a man behaved like an ass.

"Zach, ma'am." He pulled the door the rest of the way open. "Would you like to come in?"

His position gave him the full view of her first hesitant step inside and the way the dress swished around her ass. His attention rebounded to Logan, whose eagerness warred with satisfaction. He stood frozen, in mid-rise from his position at the table, his stare fixed on their date.

And he'd wanted to go play blackjack.

Closing the door, Zach blew out a long breath. His cock already ached with the idea of the next few hours, but his soul managed a fist pump. Hard-as-nails-and-down-on-himself Logan watched, transfixed, at the goddess striding into the room as though she owned it.

Hell, she already owns me. And Logan is a goner.

Chapter Two

Knocking on the door took more willpower than walking down the long, carpeted hallway from the elevators in the black Christian Louboutins with their *fuck me* red bottoms. The four-inch heels added a sharp definition to her already muscled legs. She'd been damn grateful for that uncomfortable wax job after she'd slipped on the satin and silk number that hugged every curve with just the slightest flare over her hips before it dropped down her thighs. The skirt's slit left very little of her right leg to the imagination.

The heels forced a hip-rolling saunter and despite a brief moment of discomfort, every step increased the aura of the illusion she'd sought to create. She felt almost desirable by the time she knocked on the door to 2106. One deep breath and a roll of her head later, she smiled when the door opened to a heart-stopping blond man in a white dress shirt and black pants.

Holy crap.

The four top buttons of his shirt were unbuttoned, revealing a well-muscled chest decorated by sprigs of white-blond hair. His sun-kissed face broadened into a hesitant smile, but no words came out.

"Mr. Evans?" She had little to go on beyond a brief physical description of each man and their names. The blond was Evans. The brunet would be Cavanaugh. But she hadn't caught sight of him yet.

"Zach, ma'am." He found his voice and pulled the door the rest of the way open. "Would you like to come in?"

Ordering the butterflies in her stomach to don battle gear, Jazz slid past him, almost wishing he hadn't stepped so far back. She wondered if he was as solid as he appeared. But whatever hesitation she experienced imploded when the second man in the room rose to his feet. A scar turned the left side of his mouth downward, but the right side tipped up. If she didn't know better she would have read surprise in his expression.

"Mr. Cavanaugh." She extended her hand, wanting to see if he would meet her halfway. Thankfully, he did. The weight of his hand closed on hers and a thrill skated up her arm to spread a wildfire through her insides. The mottled skin puckering his jaw and stretching down the side of his neck suggested an ugly burn, but did nothing to detract from his tanned, handsome face. If anything, it added gravitas to what might otherwise have been a sculpture of perfection.

"Jasmine." The husky intonation of her name detonated liquid heat between her thighs. Force of will kept a quiver of need from stretching down her legs. Instead, she shook his hand, enjoying the solid force of strength in his grip, but he released her too soon. Her palm itched with the urge to take his hand again.

A moment of awkward silence stretched out between the three of them. Zach joined them next to the table, sliding his hands into his pockets.

"It's nice to meet both of you." The lameness of her statement wasn't lost on her. She actually wondered what she should do next. Better yet, what she wanted them to do next.

"It's great to meet you." Zach latched onto her lame statement, buoying her. "We ordered dinner. I wasn't sure what you'd like, but we have a little bit of everything."

That explained the table with the multiple silver-lidded plates. As though galvanized by Zach's words, Logan pulled out a chair for her. The simple, gentlemanly act pinged her heart. She couldn't recall the last time one of the guys held a door for her, much less pulled out a chair. In all fairness, she wouldn't have encouraged chivalry, not in the units she commanded, much less from her classmates or other commanders whether they outranked her or not.

"Thank you." She laid the clutch purse on the side table next to the window. The thin black beaded handbag that carried her identification, some lipstick and six newly purchased condoms. Her belly rippled at the reminder of the condoms. Six seemed like an obnoxious number when she'd counted them out, she'd nearly put three of them back. Glancing from one broad-shouldered man to the other, she wished she'd brought more.

Her lips twitched, and she settled into the chair, letting Logan push the seat in gently. He circled around the table, choosing the seat farthest from her and Zach claimed the chair to her immediate right. Logan's posture corded with tension as he sat down; the action spoke of an old pain, muscles still stiff and sore. Lingering on the visible scarring, she wondered what type of accident he'd been in.

Zach interrupted her wandering thoughts. "I hope you like steak." He lifted the domed lids and set them off to the side, revealing three juicy steaks, baked potatoes, steamed vegetables, a salad and a heavy central platter filled with everything from mozzarella sticks to barbecue wings. Her stomach rumbled as she inhaled the heady combination of scents.

Both men paused mid-motion and she grinned, unabashed at her stomach's noisy cheer. "I'm starving actually. I spent the whole day in a spa being fed a steady diet of cucumber water and carrot sticks."

"Excellent. About the hungry part." Zach's grin grew. "Not

the rabbit food."

"Why all day in a spa?" Logan sat back from the table, as though leaning away from the intimacy of the meal. Despite the distance, he studied her and she wished they'd angled the chairs better so she could enjoy watching both men at the same time. Zach's easy manner, cheerful California surfer good looks were as compelling as Logan's darker, edgier countenance.

"Wine, water, beer?" Zach asked before she could answer Logan.

"Beer, actually. If you have it."

"If we have it." Zach bounded back to his feet, leaving her alone at the table with Logan. "The mini bar's fully stocked, we have Bud, Heineken, Corona...."

Watching Logan, her curiosity sheathed the lazy desires coiling around her butterflies, stilling their nervous flutters. "Corona, please. And I was in a spa all day to get ready for my date."

"With two men you've never met before." It wasn't quite a judgmental statement, but the barest flicker of uncertainty creased Logan's face.

They're as nervous as I am. The thought encouraged her, quieting the last of her nerves.

"Yes. I wanted to feel pretty." Honesty provided the best defense. An evening predicated on a fantasy deserved it.

"I hope you feel gorgeous because you look it." Zach rejoined them, setting three open bottles of Corona on the table, hesitating only when he thought to pass the bottle to her. "Did you want a glass?"

"Bottle is fine. It's colder that way." She wrapped her fingers around the long neck and sipped. Desire flared in Zach's eyes as he watched her drink. Lowering the bottle, she fought the urge to lick her lips. "Thank you. It's been a long time since I had a reason to dress up like this."

Dress blues didn't count. She looked great in them. She was all Marine when she wore them. Always a Marine, but tonight she wanted to embrace her inner woman and let her out to play.

Studying the food in front of her, she took the time to spread a napkin over her lap to protect the dress's fabric. But even as she picked up the knife and fork, Logan's steady gaze never wavered.

"Why would someone like you sign up for a one-night stand with a pair of total strangers?" No hint of subtlety softened the blunt question.

"Logan." Zach jerked around to stare at the other man.

"No, it's a fair question." She gave in to the impulse and laid a hand on Zach's arm. Muscle flexed beneath the long-sleeved shirt, heat filtering up to warm her hand. Touching him made the evening real. Interest replaced exasperation on Zach's features.

"So, why?" If Zach's censure disturbed Logan, it didn't show.

"Because I've fantasized about a ménage before. I wanted a night where I could feel like a woman, the only woman here. In my work, I travel…a lot." An understatement, but she wanted to cull the reality from her fantasy. "I don't get to date, I don't meet many men who I don't work with or who don't report to me. Why did you agree to a night with a total stranger? One who wanted a ménage?"

Logan took a long pull of beer, one elbow resting on the table. "It was his idea."

"He's not generally this much of an ass," Zach said, by way of apology. "And it was my idea. There're a few of us who signed up with the service, power in numbers and all that. A friend of ours met the woman of his dreams this way."

Tension thrummed through her and she removed her hand to reach for the fork and knife. Eating would give her something else to concentrate on. Logan's words sounded like he didn't want to be there, but the naked heat in his eyes suggested a hell of a lot more than just interest. As if on cue, both men cut into their meals.

"Are you looking for the woman of your dreams?"

"Yes."

"No."

She laughed at the dueling answers, cracking the newly wound tension coiling in her belly. *Am I really sitting in a hotel room with two of the best looking men I've seen in a long time, eating steak, drinking beer and planning to have sex with both of them?*

"Have you done this before?" She speared a piece of steak, the flavor succulent, not heavily spiced but rich, and she wondered what they would do if she stole the meat right off their plates.

"The one-night stand part?" Zach asked after a swallow. She watched the way he shaped the words with his beautiful mouth. Firm, even and strong.

"Hmm, the ménage part." Her gaze slid over the table to Logan, who jerked his attention back to his food when he caught her watching him. Yes, definitely more interested than he seemed comfortable with showing.

"A few times," Zach admitted. "But they were a long time ago."

"We don't generally share our women like we would a bottle of beer or season passes to the Rangers." Logan's gruffness undercut Zach's easy manner.

To hell with it. This is my night. See the men. Take the men. "I can imagine taking on both of you is going to be a challenge. I can't remember the last time I had good sex, much less the promise of incredible sex with two of the hottest men I've ever seen. So if I don't remember to thank you in the morning, let me say it now."

Logan jerked and Zach stared at her in wonder. Laughter surged around the desire humming through her. No hint of artifice marred their reactions. She admired both their physiques, their facial features, and paused to study their hands. Logan's fingers were long, thick and gripped his silverware tight enough to turn his knuckles white. Zach's were gentler, the fork hanging loosely.

She crossed one leg over the other and her sex clenched. She looked forward to discovering what those hands could do. But more than that, she wanted to get her own hands on the men. They were wearing far too many clothes. She'd eaten nearly half the steak, but the food lost its appeal.

"Would you two like to play a game?" She didn't know where the wanton in her came from, but she embraced it.

"Name your terms." Zach jumped on board, but Logan only raised his eyebrows. His gaze continually drifted along her face and then lowered as though drawn to the plunging neckline that offered up her breasts for inspection. Her nipples hardened at the thought, and she hoped they peeked through the silky fabric. She wanted him to know how he made her feel.

"Simple terms." Cradling the bottle between two of her fingers, she stroked her thumb around the rim. She knew the moment both of them noticed her thumb's gentle caress. "Truth or dare."

The table bumped, silverware clattering to plates.

"Dare me." Zach grinned. "Double dare."

Chapter Three

*R*eckless abandon shimmered in the air around Jasmine. Her arrival in the hotel suite struck him like a blow to the solar plexus. Exquisite. honey-colored skin, full, pouty red lips and a face capped with a whimsical sweep of black curl that caressed her face. The sexiest pixie he'd ever seen. With steel sheathed in fragility, she stood on the chair, one bare foot propped on the table. A slender silver band wrapped around her index toe beckoned him.

"I'm king of the world!" She threw her arms wide, breasts arching toward the ceiling and the strangest sensation of lightheartedness swept through him.

Logan laughed. Zach whipped around at the sound, but he ignored him. Her pose hinted at the red panties beneath her black dress. Panties that matched the red paint on her toes.

Archly, she stared at him. "Truth or dare."

She hopped down from the chair, accepting Zach's hand. She leaned into him, still grinning from the dare to play out her favorite movie part.

Logan met the snapping fire in her black eyes. They were the color of midnight, the velvety, sweet spot of night. *Oh, what the hell....* "Dare."

Still leaning against his friend, she clapped her hands

together. The playfulness stretched the scars around Logan's heart.

"I dare you to kiss me." Her throaty whisper hitched just the barest moment on the last word. His gut jerked at the challenge. He hadn't kissed a woman, not even Rochelle, since before the accident. She'd always seemed repulsed by the muscle atrophy that turned the left side of his face into a permanent frown, the pity in her expression whenever she turned at the last moment to kiss his right cheek, never his left.

Jasmine however, reflected only anticipation, humor and breathless wonder. Did the night free her to such abandon? *Is she always like this?* He found himself hoping—actually hoping—that the answer combined the two.

Zach's hand grazed along the gentle swell of her hip and Logan's gaze wandered over her curves before he lifted his right hand and beckoned her with a finger. If she wanted a kiss, she had to come and get it.

A challenge.

A gauntlet.

Damned if she didn't circle around Zach toward him. She planted one hand near his plate and the other feathered down to touch his left shoulder. Anticipation twisted through his gut, nobody touched his scars, but the heat of it pushed right through the fabric, digging deep into the scar tissue to spread warmth tumbling against the strange squeeze around his heart.

He lifted his chin a fraction in invitation. Her sinful, pink tongue flicked out to moisten her lips. A perfect cupid's bow. A year ago, he would have urged it down to his cock. Hell, he was considering that now.

Her warm breath teased his face. He smelled the sweetness of her perfume, some flowery combination that reminded him of sultry, hot Texas nights. It seemed eons passed between the dip of her head until the moment her lips caressed the corner of his mouth.

The left corner.

The damaged and permanently scarred corner.

A jolt speared him as her tongue stroked over the scar tissue. She kissed him slowly, a symphony of light, erotic sensations. He opened for her and sucked the flavor inside. The cold, practical part of his mind snorted at the clack of teeth. Hardly the kiss of an expert, but when he dared explore deeper, a shiver of awareness rippled over his skin, awakening long dormant needs.

Warm, wet heat flooded his joints, but his cock remained ever quiet, unmoved. He gave into the temptation to cup her face with his hands, fingers stroking the smoothness of her cheek. She didn't pull away and the kiss ended as slowly as it began, with nuzzling sweetness along his scars. Her gentle retreat brushed her nose against his and he steeled himself for the revulsion—or worse, the pity—he would see in her, but her heavy-lidded black eyes offered no hint of condolence.

"Wow," she murmured, and dropped a warm kiss near the corner of his eye. "Can I dare you again?"

The rusty sound of laughter wheezed out of his chest. "No, you have to wait."

Just beyond her head, Zach gave him two thumbs up. Thumbs that he immediately tucked back into his pockets as she straightened, giving Logan an eyeful of her breasts. The twin globes strained above the plunging neckline, swelling like two ripe apples, flushed to pink with need.

Logan wanted to run his fingers down the sweet V, caress the heat of her skin and roll the weight of the pert, round nipples tenting the silk fabric with his fingers. But he leashed that desire. "You need to dare Zach."

Fortunately for all of them, she dared Zach to sing. The dirty and faintly insulting lyrics of Rodney Carrington's *Put Your Clothes Back On* and country twang sent her into gales of laughter.

Zach dared her next to eat from his fingers.

Logan never imagined that watching another man feed a

woman could be so erotic. Every time she took a bite or licked the juice from Zach's fingers, Logan's skin tightened. The next dare stripped Zach of his shirt and forced a pectoral dance. Not Logan's favorite activity to watch, but her unabashed reaction created a cocktail of sexy humor.

He'd been content with the game until the kiss. A kiss he considered daring her to repeat, only straddling his quiet lap the second time around. But his cock wasn't interested and hadn't been in a long time. The nerve damage combined with fire and trauma seemed to have permanently emasculated him. Yet the daring promise in her midnight gaze beckoned him to try. He'd passed previously.

Not this time.

"I dare you," Logan began, spitting the words out before he could design a strategic retreat from the conversation, "To let *me* peel those sexy, red panties off you."

Yeah, he wanted those panties. The provocative glimpse when she perched up on the chair sparked the first sensation of heat in his gut that he'd felt in months. Besides, Zach's cock was all but ready to burst from his pants. *Might as well help a brother out.*

"Here?" she asked, but Logan shook his head and pointed to the sofa. She pivoted neatly on her bare feet, giving him a fine view of her rounded ass as she strolled toward the sofa. He rose, ignoring the stiff hitch of his left leg and forced himself to walk without a limp. The skin pulled tight, the scarring around his knee and hip inhibiting mobility, but even limited he could still move and he hadn't spent months in a physical therapist's merciless hands for nothing.

Zach retreated to the chair in the living room. They were done with dinner. Jasmine leaned against the sofa, her legs stretched out in front of her, and feet propped against the floor, toes pointed as though a ballerina, but Logan concentrated on the rapid rise and fall of her breasts.

The dare stimulated her and pleasure uncurled a fist around his heart. He might not be able to fill her with a cock, he'd have to leave that sweet task to Zach, but he could still enjoy getting her ready. She reached for her skirt as though to roll it up, but Logan shook his head.

"Hands off," he murmured. "I said let *me* take them off."

Her smile grew and her chest hitched a one-two beat before she put her hands on the back of the sofa. Nodding his approval, Logan lowered himself, a slow, halting kneel that shot an ache racing up his spine, but he ignored the pain. He wanted to be down there, he could already smell the musk of her, the salty, tang of moistness that beckoned.

Mouth dry, he steadied on his right knee and drifted his hands over her hips. The silk fabric scraped the scars on his left palm, but he found the slit that opened over her thigh and inch by inch, slid the skirt up.

The scrap of red splashed color that contrasted with her honeyed skin. Heat licked up his palms and a blush pinkened her skin just above the delicate lace, a beautiful compliment of sweet and sexy. He'd intended to hook his thumbs and tug the scrap down, but proximity gave him another idea.

He spared a glance down at his groin. *If there was ever a time to wake up, this is it.* He grazed his mouth along the waistline of the panties and her breath hitched. Skimpy fabric plastered her sweet flesh, but he found the skin just below the elastic band and sampled butterscotch and a hint of apricots.

She'd mentioned a spa earlier. A massage.

Tracing a path to her right hip, he wondered if it was edible massage oil. Closing his teeth over the silk clinging to her hip, he drew it down. Sweet, hot, damp sex filled his nostrils. Between his thighs, his cock quivered.

A quiver.

A single, brief sensation stirred the flaccid length. Biting down, Logan ripped the panties and she gasped, but he didn't pause, sweeping across her abdomen to the left side. A hint of curl teased his tongue as he passed close to the apex of her thighs. She wasn't waxed there.

A second quiver joined the first, his balls tightening as

though one of her soft palms cupped him.

Think about her, think about the taste of her. He laved at the butterscotch-kissed skin until he found the second seam. Only then did he lift his gaze upward to follow the exquisite curves of her torso and see the raw desire shimmering on her face.

He held her eyes as he ripped the second seam. The fabric slipped downward, baring the dark V of curls. He nudged her thighs apart and lapped a gentle kiss down to the pink lips that barely peeked between the curls. Sweet cream filled his mouth and her moan jerked another reaction from his cock.

A real jerk.

He slid his tongue around the hard, swollen clit he couldn't see. Her legs buckled, thighs parting. The red scrap drifted to the floor between them. Grinning, he gave the precious button a long, sucking kiss until her hands gripped his shoulders and she braced her ass to keep her from falling.

The low, keening cry of her orgasm was music to his ears and a smile creased the scars on his face when he leaned back. She tasted delicious. He could dine on her for months. Her raw, open reaction stirred more life in him than he'd experienced since the roadside bomb ended his career, his passion and damn near took his life.

"Your turn." He glanced up the flushed length of her, barely recognizing the husky sound as his own voice, her scent drugging his senses.

"Actually," Zach leaned over the sofa, grinning. "It's mine."

ca

Zach needed to send that Madame Eve person about two dozen roses, maybe some chocolates and whatever the hell else might be the appropriate gift for giving someone back his best friend. In the two hours since Jasmine arrived, Logan— his Logan—returned to fill out the shell of the man who'd woken up in the German hospital bed nine months before. Not even taking his first real steps afterward had filled the man with life.

No, this is all her.

His gaze whisked over her dewy face, parted lips and the rapid rise and fall of her chest. He grinned broader. He'd been at attention since she'd walked in, but right then, he could kiss every single toe on her foot. She'd made Logan smile. She'd kissed his scarred face and she'd come apart with his mouth on her.

Zach could worship her like a goddess just for that. Propping his elbows on the sofa, he'd damn near came all over himself watching her orgasm. Her reactions were so real her surprise mixing with want, need mingling with desire. No artifice. No posing.

His woman.

No. He cocked an eyebrow at Logan's lazy grin. *Our woman.*

Stealing a glance down her length to the downy, black fur between her thighs, his cock flexed. He wanted to taste her, but right then all he wanted was to be balls deep, driving into the wet heat and filling her to the brim. He wanted to drive into her until she screamed and then he wanted to come. Bareback would be preferable, but he had plenty of condoms.

They could work up to the rest.

"So, truth?" He stroked a finger down the length of her arm, enjoying the quiver of flesh and the wide-eyed stare she cast in his direction.

"It's truth or dare." She licked her lips.

He chuckled, continuing the lazy trace of his fingers. He loved the smoothness of her skin, the warmth, the definition. Every muscle defined without an ounce of spare flesh. If God set out to build a perfect woman, He'd struck gold with Jasmine.

"Yeah, I know. But I want you to pick truth."

"Truth, then." Her voice whispered across him. He wished she'd dared him to strip his pants earlier. The lack of shirt hardly bothered him. But his pants threatened to geld him.

"Do you really want to have sex with us?" Careful to use the word us, he didn't miss Logan's narrowed eyes or the laser beam stare he focused on her face. "Both of us, together, apart, at the same time, one at a time, however we want to have you?"

Zach wanted the answer. He needed the answer. She seemed to enjoy his attention, but her interest focused on Logan. *If she wants Logan by himself, I'm out.* His cock protested, but he ignored it. The night was about Logan.

Truth be told, it was about Logan and Jasmine now, but whatever she wanted, Zach and Logan would both give it to her.

"Yes," she murmured, so low he barely heard her.

"Yes?" He trailed his fingers to her collarbone, stroking the pulse point where her neck met her shoulder. It pounded beneath his fingertips. "Yes to what?"

"Just yes. Together. Apart. One at a time. At the same time. I want to have sex with both of you." Absolute, unabashed honesty filled her tone and her skin turned rosy. He loved that blush.

The most sensual creature he'd ever encountered, he hoped she never stopped doing it. She blushed prettier than a high school cheerleader being asked out on her first date. Glancing at Logan, Zach shifted along the back of the sofa to let his hand rub in slow circles down beneath the fabric of her dress. His palm grazed a pointed nipple and the round suppleness of her breast filled his hand.

Perfect.

"You heard that, right Logan? She said both of us."

Logan's pleasant surprise snapped the last doubt in Zach's mind. "She did."

Massaging her breast, Zach leaned forward and caught her mouth in an open, wet, hot kiss. He thrust his tongue inside, mirroring the desire of his cock to be buried there. He could imagine sliding his cock between her lips, holding her hair as he pounded toward release. But time for that later. He had tighter, wetter ideas in mind.

He found the clasp on the back of her dress and released it, rolling her nipple between his thumb and forefinger as the fabric whispered downward. He sensed more than saw Logan peeling the dress off and then she was nude, completely, gloriously naked, her body everything the dress promised from the supple curves of her breasts to the narrow, flat plane of her belly.

Breaking the kiss, he glanced up. "New plan. We need the bedroom."

"Agreed." Logan surged to his feet, scooping her up. Her bottom lifted to Zach's eye level and he nipped one cheek. *I'm not going to last.*

Logan barely limped as he carried her into the bedroom. Zach grabbed the condoms out of his back pocket and tossed his wallet onto the coffee table before crowding right behind them.

"Better suit up, Marine," he murmured to himself, ripping open one package and unbuckling his belt. Jasmine's hands dug into Logan's biceps, her face squeezed tight as he kissed the hell out of her. Zach never thought of himself as a voyeur, but his stiff cock sprang free from his pants, as eager as he to sample her, already on her knees.

Kicking off his pants, he rounded the bed and slid up behind her. He rolled the condom on, the cool tightness doing little to dampen the raging need pounding the head of his cock. The mattress dipped under their weight and she wiggled her ass when he stroked his hands over the curves. It was so round, so warm and he palmed the cheeks, skimming her anus and lower still until he found the parted lips of her sex, wet and hot, and glided his fingers right into her. She clenched around him and he had to work to spread her wider, readying her, because once his cock slid inside, it wasn't going to be a patient, gentle fuck.

"Help me," he murmured through clenched teeth, pushing

deeper, stretching. Logan dropped his hand down between her thighs, nudging them apart. He broke from the kiss, urging until she bent forward. Logan's coaxed her clit and her hard, shallow pants turned into sharp, gasps of sound.

God, I hope she's ready. He withdrew and licked the taste of her from his hand with a moan. Her whimper of need dragged him back to the moment. He positioned his sheathed cock, his hands falling to her hips and then he slid inside until his balls stretched unbearably with the need to release.

His hips rolled, one thrust and her slick, tight heat closed like a fist around him. Her moan lit his insides. He drew back and thrust again, balls slapping against her mound.

"Yes!" Her exclamation pulled his orgasm from him like a bolt of lightning, riding up his cock and he fought the urge to orgasm. Her anus winked at him and his cock jerked. Would she let him between her ass cheeks, would she take him there while Logan filled her sweet sex?

The image undid him—he'd never been an ass man before. *Thank God Logan is working her clit.* She came apart underneath him, hips surging back to meet every thrust as he came with her.

Chapter Four

Oh God, this really is happening....

The lucid thought punched through the haze of desire wrapping around her. Logan's hot tongue and scraping teeth on her sex flooded her with desire until she came. When Zach had stroked up her arm and asked if she really wanted them, she nearly wept all over again. She'd never experienced two orgasms that close together, much less on the heels of the first. They were both still wearing too many clothes and except for the heat of Zach's hard callused palm massaging her breast and Logan's warm, moist breath on her sex, they'd barely touched her.

"Yes!" And then Logan picked her up. A strong woman, she could bench press two hundred and fifty pounds, handle a fifty caliber and still held the best time for the urban obstacle course at Camp Lejeune, but their pure masculinity dwarfed her. In Logan's arms, she felt soft, feminine and all woman. She'd stolen a kiss on the way to the bedroom, barely glimpsing Zach's determined expression as he followed them. The sound of his pants hitting the floor sent a sensual thrill tingling through her thighs. For one brief moment, she worried she'd peed, but then Zach's hands were on her ass, the tormenting bite he'd pressed to it, drawing her need taut. She wanted him inside her. She wanted both of them.

Logan pulled away from her kiss and she moaned at the loss of it. The fingers filling her sent electricity racing up her spine and then Logan stroked his thumb over her sex. Her hands fell to the bed, fingers digging into the bed sheet. She rocked between them, aching with need. Zach's hand slid away and she whimpered.

Why did he stop?

But then his cock nudged her entrance and she strained back to meet it. His hard thrusts stretched her, pain and pleasure twining. He was incredible, driving deep into her, the friction delicious and she wanted more. Logan's hand continued to flick, roll and rub her clit. Her nipples burned with every brush of his arm, the fabric of his shirt rasping across one, tormenting it and leaving the other aching for a similar touch.

She twisted along his arm, pressing her hips back in invitation to Zach. Stretching forward until eye level with his groin, she glared at his clothes.

More...

The errant thought drowned in a torrent of feeling as a second orgasm spiraled through her belly, shooting jets of liquid heat through her muscles. Zach's answering groan filled her and his cock vibrated inside of her. Struggling with raging need, she reached for Logan's belt and worked it free, the buttons and zippers no challenge versus the drive to touch him, taste him.

His fingers halted and she felt, more than saw him begin to pull away. Tilting her head back, she shook it in mutiny.

"Let me touch you, please." The raw, wanton voice didn't belong to her, but the plea worked. Logan hesitated, but stayed still as she tugged his pants and simple black boxers down. Zach's hands stroked her back, his softened cock still pressed deeply within her and she divided her focus, squeezing his cock with kegels. Who knew that exercise would ever be so useful? He caressed her spine with delicate nips and gentle kisses. A wandering finger rimmed her anus.

Laughter shuddered out of her. She'd wanted to experience every sexual opportunity, to be a woman. Tingles of pleasure stroked through her. Her nerve endings sizzled and every pulse of her heart sent another wave of bliss skating over her skin. She felt beautiful, exquisite and utterly feminine.

Logan finished kicking off his pants and boxers and yanked his shirt over his head. The mottled skin she'd glimpsed along his neck and hand ran all the way down his side. His left thigh puckered with the twisted scarring of burnt flesh. Pain for him rolled through the cloud of pleasure holding her body hostage. Pain for the agony these injuries must have cost him. Pain for the stiffness of his posture.

Behind her, Zach eased away, but she let him go without comment. Wonder filled her as she looked up the length of Logan's body, meeting his closed expression. He expected rejection.

He is about to be disappointed.

Stretching forward, she kissed the scarred skin of his hip. She parted her lips, her tongue gliding over the rough ridges. A surgical scar dimpled the mottled flesh and she stroked a caress along the length of it. She rose and watched his face. He braced himself, desire peeking through his caution. Kissing her way down the chest, she laved attention to the scarred and the unscarred skin. The hard muscle beneath her fingers trembled, but she indulged herself. She wanted to touch him.

She wanted to taste him.

She wanted to give back that pleasure he'd given her in the sitting room. At his groin, she massaged the softened length of cock. She didn't know what led to his accident or how he'd earned the scars decorating the left side of his body, but she recognized the trauma, the fear and the reluctance. Lapping gently around the head of his flaccid cock, she tasted fear. She eased the length between her lips, careful not to hurt him with her teeth.

The bed dipped behind her and a warm, wet wash cloth stroked her sex. Her heart thudded like an eager puppy, delighted at Zach's return. Rolling Logan's cock around in her mouth, she gently sucked the head. Emboldened by his sharp inhale, she used one hand to brace herself and the other to cup his balls. A turgid lift of skin told her the scars had spread out to try and emasculate him, but he remained whole.

Even if he didn't feel that way. A drop of fluid beaded along the head of his cock and she paused in mid-stroke to lick the slit, drawing out the flavor. Quivers rolled up his length, the member stiffening. Pure delight filled her as she drew him deep.

Logan's fingers fisted in her hair as his cock engorged. It strained her jaws, and she opened wider, stroking the hardening length with every lick. His balls swelled under her hand. His thighs shook with effort and she bobbed her head forward, encouraging him to thrust. Behind her, Zach washed her sex gently.

It was all she could do not to push back. Logan's hands tightened in her hair, his cock thrusting deep and she swallowed, tasting his desire, richer than the steak they'd dined on. Her gaze skittered up and he stared at her with wonder, the wariness gone.

"I want...." he began and she eased back then, bumping Zach.

"What do you want?" she asked, favoring the thick, red head of his cock with another kiss.

"You." He withdrew, and Zach flipped her onto her back and tossed a condom to him. Jasmine stared at them, dazed at the swift change in position then gasped when Logan lifted her thighs, spread her wide and sank into her.

Sensitive and swollen from Zach, she was barely prepared for the thick length stretching her. Logan adjusted their position until her calf rested against his neck. Zach stretched out to next to her on the bed and tilted her chin, kissing her. The hint of stubble on his cheeks added another layer of sensation to the sensual assault on her body and Logan surged.

Zach's kiss stole her breath even as Logan's cock pounded deep enough to knock on her womb. Her insides turned to liquid and she came, crying out Logan's name and then Zach's. That pulled the last of her sanity with it and she arched up, her gaze colliding with Logan's. His face twisted into a grimace of pleasure and his cock jerked as he came.

He slipped away, but Zach pulled her toward him, stroking, tormenting and urging her until she came again. Hands drifted over her body, mouths tormented her nipples, Zach wrapped her fingers around his cock. She stroked him to hardness again and then he was inside her. They cradled her and drew out her orgasm. They took turns stretching and filling her until she thought she'd explode from delight. Drunk on pleasure, they collapsed.

They took breaks for food, more beer and laughter.

So much laughter.

She rose up above Logan, rode him, watched Zach stroke his own cock back to life. Arching her head back, she laughed to the ceiling.

I am woman. Hear me roar....

Logan leaned up on an elbow. Every joint in his body protested at the position, but he wanted to watch her sleep. She'd snuggled between them and drifted off a little after three in the morning. Her nipples were swollen and distended, reddened from their lavish attention. The room reeked of sex.

The sweet scent of Jasmine covered him. He could still taste her cream. He'd taken her twice and seriously considered a third go, but she slept so soundly, so sweetly it left him loathe to wake her.

His cock ached from friction, but the twitch of motion against his thigh delighted him. He'd thought she'd be repulsed when she'd seen the scars. Seen the way they twisted his skin, disfiguring him. He wasn't Zach with a physique to match his sunny disposition, but she'd kissed his scars, taken his flaccid, useless cock and teased life back into him.

That first orgasm damn near blinded him. He'd hardly expected a second, a third or a fourth. Her ass was tighter than her sex, but she'd taken him, every hard inch as he'd glided along the narrow passage. Across the bed, Zach shifted and mirrored Logan's pose, propping his head on his hand.

"Better?" Stupid question, but his best friend had a right to ask it. *To think I considered playing blackjack as an alternative to this.*

"Oh, yeah. I owe you."

"Nope, you don't." Zach trailed a finger down her side and frowned.

"What?"

"Bullet scar." Worry threaded through Zach's voice and Logan leaned forward to examine the puckered mark along the right side of her abdomen. "A through and through."

Zach was right. The scar mirrored a second one on her back. The bullet grazed the side of her belly, just an inch lower and it could have punctured her intestines. Quiet anger stirred inside of him, rousing from a year of slumber in the cave of apathy.

He met Zach's gaze and both men shifted, examining the rest of her. A knife mark showed on one calf and second puckered mark revealed a bullet scar along her left collarbone. Logan planned to find out what sonofabitch took a shot at her and snap every bone in his hand before he snapped his neck.

"Iraq." Her drowsy voice halted their inspection.

Logan's heart squeezed.

She stretched her arms out, reaching first for him and then to Zach, her fingers curling to caress their cheeks. "A sniper.

But we got him. So you don't have to look so pissed."

"What were you doing in Iraq?" Zach asked the question that echoed through Logan.

"Assignment. Did I mention I'm a Gunnery Sergeant?"

Holy hell. She's a Marine.

"Active?" Zach's voice tightened on the question.

"I meet with my CO in the morning."

"You're going back?" Logan frowned. He didn't know whether to laugh or shake her. *Is she out of her mind?*

"Yes." Her voice cooled. "I'm a Marine."

Logan's gaze cut up to meet Zach's. Marines went back. They went where they were needed. If the Corps would let him, he'd go back, too. But they'd discharged him on permanent disability.

"Well, I guess it was too good to last." She began to sit up and as one, they pushed her back down.

"Night's not over, sweetheart." Zach grinned and the wariness edging Jasmine's expression eased.

"No?" She flicked a look between them.

"No," Logan agreed and slid his hand right down to her still wet sex, and drove two fingers into her, enjoying the way her eyes widened. "You just caught us off guard."

Her mouth formed a little circle as Logan began to stroke her gently, probing the swollen flesh of her sex with two fingers. She wouldn't forget tonight.

Ever.

"Yep," Zach agreed, kissing a path along her cheek. "But surprise doesn't mean retreat."

"Are you on leave?" Logan stroked a thumb around her clit, not quite touching it. When her hips lifted, his hand retreated and she moaned. "Answer the question."

Zach licked across the red rosette of one nipple and blew a breath, adding to her agony. Logan waited until her hips stilled to press a third finger into the hot flesh of her sex.

"Two weeks. My unit deploys on Friday, but my CO wanted me to have the time to consider whether I wanted to remain active or not." Hard panting punctuated the words. Logan rewarded her answer with a roll of his thumb over her clit. She bowed her back as Zach favored her nipple with his teeth, dragging it upward.

"Nice," Logan complimented him. "You want top or bottom this time?"

"I want her mouth," Zach commented. "I want her to swallow every inch of me. If that's all right with you, ma'am."

Logan laughed at her strangled gasp, scooting down her body to press a long, vibrating kiss to her clit. She bucked her hips and he pinched her ass in reprisal. "If you move, I stop."

"Not fair."

"Nope. But this isn't about fair." Her musk teased his nostrils. He really could get drunk on her. "This is about making sure you don't forget us."

"I don't think that will be a problem," she chuckled, her sex quivering invitingly up at him.

"Then I have one condition." Zach shifted on the bed, edging up near her face, his cock in full salute.

"Name it." She didn't blink, her gaze fastened on Zach's midsection and Logan nipped her clit, dragging her attention back to him. They'd shared women before, a quick fuck, a night of fun, and never looked back. But Jasmine was *different*. Zach's tone told Logan that he felt the same way. He didn't mind sharing her with Zach, as long as they were on the same page.

"Your next leave belongs to us."

Hell yes they were on the same page. Logan had forgotten what being whole was like, what it was to be a man. He wasn't giving that up. He wasn't giving up Zach's part in it either. Watching the two of them, watching Zach fill her, lit the match.

"Both of us," Logan agreed, swirling his tongue around the swollen nub. "You just tell us when...."

"...and we'll be there." Zach feathered his fingers over her cheek and lower to cup her neck.

"Both of you." She pressed a kiss to the swollen tip of Zach's cock and Logan grinned.

Semper fi....

No Regrets,
No Surrender

Chapter One

*I*t was damn hot in the sandbox. In the town of Bamyan, a cluster of mud brick homes huddled together under the merciless sun. Temperatures soared close to ninety degrees, a heat wave for the region, despite the lateness of the afternoon. Jazz's sunglasses barely filtered the blinding glare off the sand and camel-colored buildings when she and the other members of the FET or Female Engagement Team arrived in the MRAP armored fighting vehicle at dawn.

Her tan MARPATs were dusty with sand. The grit seemed to get into everything. The Bamyan province was designated a mountainous region, but it didn't feel like one today. In addition to Jazz, her three-woman unit consisted of Mary "Stormer" Phillips and Roxanne "Roxy" Cortez. She'd written to Zach and Logan the other day that she never imagined two women more different than she, yet they'd developed an instant rapport.

Stormer's mocha-colored skin and Amerasian features combined to make her a stunner. She may have turned down a career as a brilliant runway model, but she made an excellent Marine. Roxy was born in Puerto Rico and descended from Cuban immigrants with a little Russian to give her Latin looks a pair of the most incredible blue eyes.

Jazz took a picture of the three of them and planned to email it the next chance she got. Ten months since she'd enjoyed a rapturous night of fantasy in Las Vegas, she missed Zach and Logan more every day. It might as well have been ten years. She'd managed a weekend escape to Germany. Four days of bliss with Logan spent naked and hot, then another brief three days in Italy, but only Zach made it over for that trip.

Today's exercise required sitting inside a private classroom at the University of Bamyan. Their audience was a group of Afghani girls whose American counterparts would be trying out for cheerleading at home. These girls and their mothers were as far removed from those experiences as possible. Jazz's team had been making the rounds throughout the region, inviting women to the university's slowly restored campus in an effort to engage them with academic possibilities, while learning more about their needs. Stormer led today's conversation.

Most of the women, even in the larger cities, wouldn't talk to the U.S. military's male representatives. The FET relied on the double-X chromosome of its Marines to bridge that cultural barrier. Currently, they experienced a forty percent success rate. They'd invited over a hundred women—forty had shown up.

They'd seen fewer.

"Jazz?" Stormer's nudge pulled her from her internal musings. Many of the older women wore veils across their faces despite the region's Buddhist history, thanks to the influence of the Taliban. The younger girls dropped their veils as soon as they had entered the building, but maintained their head scarves or *hijab*. Unlike their mothers, the teens dressed in brighter, vibrant colors—exotic birds amidst the drab.

"We want to help provide the education you wish to have." Jazz used Pashtu, the most commonly spoken language in the region. Even those who didn't speak it fluently understood it. Even with her bad accent.

A couple of the younger girls snickered, the sound so reminiscent of the way a teen should sound, Jazz's heart ached. An older woman silenced the giggling pair with a stern look, but Jazz simply smiled. "We understand that our ways are not yours. While we can make recommendations based on our studies, we believe in self-determination. We want to know what you as mothers wish for your daughters, and what your daughters wish for themselves. We've restored much of the university, and we can help arrange for instructors—female instructors, if you wish—in areas of agriculture, writing, reading, science. Whatever you want to study, we can find a way to make that happen."

Two or three of the younger girls leaned forward. The motion was nearly imperceptible, but she saw interest glint in their gazes. If they reached only one girl, these missions were considered a success. The mothers kept their expressions neutral, save for one, who glanced at her daughter with regret.

She wanted that for her child. An opportunity Jazz might pursue to keep the dialogue open. The meetings always began with Roxy introducing them, describing their mission, and setting the women at ease. She possessed that motherly quality in addition to being proficient with fifty-caliber guns and a master at hand-to-hand combat. After Roxy, Stormer typically took over to work on the logistics of how such an education benefited the girls.

Jazz was the closer. She read people almost as well as she did inventory reports. She knew which girls to target afterward, and when to gently leverage the pressure in order to help them overcome the innate fear of change. The brutal heel of the Taliban continued to press down on their necks long after the regime was on the run.

She could cheerfully string up every hypocritical bastard who'd constructed a system of government that classified its women somewhere below its goats.

Because they sure as hell treated the goats better.

Focusing on the turquoise-outfitted teen, Jazz leaned back

against the desk. Her team tried not to stand or pace. Their standard flak jackets and fatigues created a worrisome enough effect, but their ability to be casual earned them greater access to the secluded minds that fought against hope.

"Badria, your name means moonlike."

Happiness lightened the girl's expression. Yes, Jazz had paid attention to their murmured introductions. "The moon is something we study in our science classes and in astronomy. We look to the skies and study the heavens, the stars, the planetary bodies and the universe as a whole, so we can better understand ourselves."

"The moon is lovely." Badria's shy smile widened. "I used to chart its path and its shape to help my mother when I was little."

"When I was little, I used to climb up onto the roof of my house and stare up at the sky. I would try to pick out all the visible constellations and count the stars. I thought if I could count every star in the sky, I would never be lost." Jazz gave them an encouraging smile.

"But the number of stars are infinite...." This from the young Anoonseh who wasn't more than twelve. She ducked away from her mother's admonishing arm to sidle closer to Badria. "How can you count them all?"

Jazz lifted her hands. "I couldn't, but that didn't stop me from trying. In some of our cities, the light is so bright that we cannot see the stars. Sometimes we forget that they are there."

"You can see them everywhere here." Anoonseh nodded with the arrogance only a child possessed. "We are better than America, we have more stars."

Grinning, Jazz slid off the desk and sat down on the floor. "Yes, you do have more stars. Do you like to study the sky, too, Anoonseh?"

"No. I like animals. I want to know how to help them. We lost our cow when her baby would not turn and Tinsah, who knew how to take care of the cow's problem, was too far away. She is in so much demand."

"So you want to learn to be a veterinarian?" That didn't surprise Jazz. In most of the rural communities, the women had more rights than they did in the cities—and in many cases more skills. Since men were forbidden to mingle with women, even in rural areas, the females had to learn how to tend their animals themselves, to care for them and provide medical support if necessary.

"Yes!" Anoonseh bobbed her head but as easily as the excitement rippled across her face, it diminished. "The classes are in Pakistan and I cannot travel that far alone."

"Perhaps not, but what if we were to bring some female veterinarians here? Would your mother allow you to attend those classes?" It was a careful balancing act to offer freedom with jesses attached. While Jazz addressed the question to Anoonseh and kept her focus on her, she carefully watched her mother staring at the young girl. She definitely wanted it, too.

"If you bring other teachers for science, I will take Anoonseh to veterinarian class, and she can come to my science class and to Shara's class on teaching. She wishes to become a teacher. Fadwah wishes to learn the counting skills, so she can manage our village's money." Badria took a stand and Jazz knew they had them. She'd included many of the girls from her village, creating a community effort. The mothers shifted silently, but hopeful looks passed among them.

They wanted to take advantage of the offers.

"Do any of you know how to write?" As planned, she, Stormer and Roxy stood and collected writing pads and pencils they'd brought with them. Two or three hands rose— including one tentative mother's—and they passed out the supplies to them. "We will leave you to consider what classes you most wish for, if you will write down your requirements, we can get to work on that for you right away. We would also like contact information. If you write down that information for those who do not know how to write, we can make sure you know when the opportunities will begin."

No one began writing immediately and likely wouldn't

until they stepped out. Jazz swept another look across the gathering. Gone was the stiff reserve, leaving only wary optimism and curiosity behind. Stormer jerked her chin at the door and Roxy nodded. Jazz picked up her helmet and gathered her gear. They would leave the women to it. The brave and the interested would turn in the information at the designated drop spots, to be gathered later.

Jazz exited the room's nonexistent air-conditioning and a faint breeze cooled the sweat slicking the back of her neck.

"Nice job."

"Back atcha."

The compliments were the only pats on the back they allowed themselves as they donned helmets to match their flak. They'd been closeted with those women for most of the day and had a long drive to get back to base, report in and clean up. Roxy shipped for home in three days for a well-deserved, two-week leave with her kids. Jazz and Stormer would work recon in the villages they'd been to previously, reconnecting with potential students. So far of the five hundred or so women they'd engaged in the last four months, thirty were signed up for the first round of university classes.

"Sar-shent Wind-ers!" Anoonseh raced up the hallway toward the courtyard they were exiting. Jazz waved the other two women onward and turned back to the girl. "My list. I wrote it myself."

She skidded to a halt a couple of feet away, waving a sheet of yellow legal pad paper, her excitement dimming as she took in the full picture of Jazz's uniform. The helmet's rounded head gave her a harder edge and helped to disguise her feminine features. From a distance, the only thing that distinguished her from her male Marine counterparts was her height.

And only if the guys with her were giants—like Logan and Zach. Pushing aside that thought, Jazz pulled her helmet off. She wasn't quite outside yet, but the tension in Anoonseh's expression immediately relaxed. Jazz didn't take a step toward her, or the scarlet bird might race back the way she came.

"May I see it?"

Stormer and Roxy retreated to a safe distance and would wait for her before entering the MRAP, giving Anoonseh a modicum of privacy. They were alone in the silent hallway with only a breeze for company.

The young girl edged forward shyly and held out the list, a single, crinkled sheet written in Pashtu. Jazz spoke it better than she read it, but she recognized several words. The items nearly covered the length of the page.

"Thank you. I will work on this for you," she promised.

A vibrating buzz whispered in the air. Ice clutched her heart and she reacted, lunging forward and scooping the little girl up and flinging her through an open doorway. Blinding light filled the shadowed hall and darkness swallowed her.

ઈ

Whistle balanced between his lips, Zach blew a warning as Fin body-blocked third base with his foot on the sandbag. The third baseman caught the ball and tagged Jace as his scrawnier opponent slid in, riding a wave of red sand. The collision ended with Jace leaping up and throwing the first punch and the boys pummeling each other. Zach shot forward from his position between third and home plate on the intercept and blew the whistle again.

Son of a bitch.

With nearly fifty pounds on the batter, Fin was more wrestler than pugilist. He pinned the smaller kid. But Jace's Navy SEAL father apparently taught his son more than one trick, and the kid flipped the older teen and blocked a punch beautifully with a slide of his forearm to turn the fist away.

Unlike most teams that might have started the rallying cry of *fight, fight, fight*, their teammates fell back a step as Zach waded in. The stiffening of shoulders and spines coupled with the rigid hold of their positions were a credit to their military parents and the rules of the game.

Jace and Fin were about to be in the boob box, and no one else wanted to join them. Zach easily caught Jace's next punch, twisted the fourteen-year-old's arm behind his back, and planted his free hand against Fin's chest.

"Stand down." His order rang across the rapidly warming May morning and echoed with command. As coach, Zach was a favorite among the players for his cheerful, encouraging attitude, and firm patience. He didn't bend rules and he didn't give them slack. Teenagers needed boundaries and expectations. His kids knew what would happen and respected those rules.

Most of the time.

Fin drove forward against the hand on his chest and challenged him. It was Zach's job to hold that line and he twisted, using Fin's own weight against him as he flipped and pinned him.

"Stand. Down."

The order penetrated that time. Panting for breath, Jace held up his hands and backed off. Fin opened his fists, palms out, and Zach released the pressure on his chest. He rose from the crouch and folded his arms across his chest. Fin's glove lay next to third base, ball still cupped in the mitt, their caps three feet away. He surveyed their red-dusted uniforms with a hard, critical eye.

"On your feet."

Fin scrambled to stand. They stayed away from each other. Jace's right eye looked puffy and showed the early signs of bruising. Fin's split lip dripped blood onto his white uniform top.

"He blocked the base—"

"The little prick was out—"

Zach raised his hand and the deluge of words cut off as quickly as it began. "Explain honor, Jace."

The young man sucked in a breath. Thirty teenagers ranging in age from thirteen to seventeen were on campus at

Mike's Place for the summer. Zach had invited them to sign up for the baseball team over spring break, and training began the first of April. They planned games against other regional boys' teams to kick off in two weeks. He'd demanded only three very specific rules from his team and its motley crew of military sons.

"Honor requires the ultimate standard in ethical and moral conduct." Despite his slighter build, the boy's voice was deep.

"Which means what, Fin?" Zach flicked a look at the taller boy.

"We must never lie, never cheat, never steal—" Fin squirmed and hesitated.

Zach waited, never relaxing his expression. "And…?"

"And we must be accountable for our actions and hold others accountable for theirs. We must never sully our honor or the honor of others," Jace finished.

Zach hid a wince at the crack in the teen's rapidly maturing voice. "Exactly. Did either of you act with honor?"

"He was out. Fair and square—"

"He blocked the base. I touched the sandbag before he touched me with that ball."

The two glared threateningly at each other but held their positions under their leader's stare.

"I did not ask you what happened on the play. I asked you if you acted with honor."

He waited. Feet shuffled and inch by inch, their defiant looks drooped.

Jace cleared his throat. "No, sir."

Fin concurred. "No, sir." Despite his pride, his chin ducked down in a conspicuous swallow.

It was hard to be a teenager. Boys in bodies destined to become men. The struggle between comfort and discipline would be ongoing for their parents, their teachers, and their coaches. Going easy on them would do them no favors. Like all their teammates, one or both parents were active or recently retired military. Some, like Fin, saw their fathers intermittently between missions, and others, like Jace, would never see their fathers again. It was hard to serve.

It was harder to be the family of those who served.

"Fifty laps. Both of you. Go."

The boys grabbed their caps and took off at a jog, side-by-side, to loop the outer field.

Glancing at the rest of the team, Zach whistled. "Catching practice for the defense, twenty minutes. Batters, head to the cages and work on those swings."

The kids scrambled to comply, but he stayed where he was at third base, his attention equally divided between the assignments.

Logan jogged up at an easy lope, his limp barely noticeable after months of continuous therapy and training. "They're going to be best friends."

"Probably." Zach grunted, resisting the urge to grin at the thought. Right then, when the kids looked at him, they needed to see stern disapproval. How many times had he and Logan pounded the snot out of each other at the same age? He'd relax his facial expression and let the approval show in a few laps.

"You want to grab a beer when they're done?" Logan bent down to claim Fin's glove, tossed the ball up and caught it with a twist. The scars on the left side of his mouth pulled down in a grimace. It was obvious his arm still gave him problems, the scar tissue having reduced his flexibility.

"Yup. Rangers are up against Yankees."

"Sounds good." The ball continued its up and down motion as Logan tossed with his right hand and caught it behind his back with his left.

"PT is gonna kick your ass if you strain your wrist." A cool observation, nothing more, but Zach kept a watch on the ticks of strain in Logan's face.

"Eh, not warmed up enough. I need the practice and Quinton's idea of PT is observing the hill until the Marines get there to actually take it."

He didn't laugh at the comment. Like his teens, Logan needed the same kind of firm restraint, but in the twenty-two months since his injury, he'd defied all expectations on recovery. He may never have the full flexibility he boasted before being trapped in a burning Humvee, with a leg shattered and arm broken while fire burned through the layers of his skin, but he was damn close.

Because he didn't observe the hill. He took it.

"Yeah, but he's still your CO where this is concerned. Be careful he doesn't sic Doc on you." In addition to being a close friend and a member of their unit, retired PFC James Westwood was Logan's trauma counselor and despite his recovery, the two still met professionally at least once every other week.

"Yes, mother." Logan smirked and curved the ball in an easy toss at Zach.

Jace and Fin were on their tenth lap and laughter shook their sullen expressions free. Zach dropped back about ten steps and pitched the ball to Logan. His arm gave a little twinge at the wind up. He hadn't warmed up either.

"How was the meeting?" He adjusted to keep watch on his players, but they were all working well, faces lined with concentration and actually giving advice to each other. In eight weeks of training, they'd finally begun to forge the bonds of teamwork that would help them when they competed.

"We're going to be busy. Captain Dexter got the grant. We'll be expanding the physical therapy wing first, and Doc can bring in more counselors. We're also now classified a trauma one center for returning vets. Ten new families are en route. Within the year, we're going to have at least two Army specialists and one Air Force to work with. He also closed the deal on the land across the highway. We'll be adding off-campus houses for the long-term staff."

"Holy hell." Zach caught the ball and held it for a moment. "I guess he wasn't kidding."

Mike's Place was the brainchild of the captain. The facility provided first class physical and emotional therapy for wounded military and support for their families. The goal was not only reintegration into civilian life, but the healing of any injuries incurred during service. The inclusion of families was an important component.

"Nope. He's a man on a mission, and Rebecca's got a lot of talent when it comes to helping him put those plans in motion. Throw the damn ball." Logan glared at him.

Zach flung it back. He'd followed him to Mike's Place for Logan's therapy after their discharge from active duty. Initially, his focus was to get him back on his feet, but they'd discovered a calling there. Logan worked with the difficult PT patients and understood them because he was one of them. The scars on the left side of his body were a mottled collection of hard ridges. Pins secured the major joints in his left leg and his elbow.

He'd learned to walk and function again, thanks to Mike's Place. Now he paid that forward to the men and women who needed similar tough love. The final crown to his recovery, though, happened in Las Vegas and currently served in Afghanistan.

An image of Jazz's sexy, sensual grin flirted across Zach's mind, and he clamped down on the heat that flooded through him. The last thing he needed was tented shorts on the field. The right corner of Logan's mouth quirked upward. Yeah, his best friend didn't miss much.

"She didn't call last night, did she?"

They'd both worked late, crunching the last of the numbers for their estimates to complete the Captain's report. The two shared a three-bedroom apartment in the sprawling campus' residential section. Zach had left before dawn to pick up the uniforms for the team and then hit the field with them by mid-morning.

"Nope. But she and the FET were heading out for meetings so it may be a couple of days before she's got a secure line to make a call."

Of all the women to meet, they'd fallen for a Marine. For one wild night in Vegas, they'd shared her. Zach had signed them up for that one-night stand to help Logan overcome a huge hurdle in his recovery—impotence. It more than worked.

They were both hooked on her. Logan got to see her in Germany over a long weekend while Zach covered his PT shifts. Logan repaid that debt three months earlier, helping out with the kids' sports teams while Zach jetted to meet her in Italy. Just thinking about those three nights was enough to set his blood on fire.

Jazz was as beautiful as she was tough. She'd recently taken the position with FET. He'd argued with her—she was safer in the green zone, running logistics and keeping track of the hundred or so who reported to her. But she wanted to help the people they were working with and, as a woman, uniquely suited to reach out to those most harmed not only by their oppressors but the war in general.

He didn't like it, but he couldn't fault her logic. Fluent in six languages, she had skills. She also knew how to handle herself, a fact she'd proven when she dropped him on his ass and had her way with him in the middle of an argument. Laughter fisted in his throat and he chuckled. The boys were at lap thirty, sweating, and not talking so much as grunting encouragement to each other.

They'd be fast friends again and too damn tired to throw a punch by the next day.

"Stop thinking about her, man. Your face is doing the gooey-eyed thing." Logan's reminder was an easy jest, but his own guarded expression revealed similar thoughts. Jazz was not the kind of woman a man forgot—for either of them. "How much longer on her contract?"

"Eight months." The ball zinged back and forth between them. "But she's loving this new assignment."

"Yeah, I get that. She likes helping and she likes working with the people." What remained unsaid was their understanding her need to serve—they shared the same need. But they also wanted her home, and it was the unspoken thorn upsetting an otherwise great balance they'd found in sharing her.

"She can help people here." In his bed or Logan's or their shared bed, however she wanted to work that piece out. Zach didn't mind sharing with his best friend. Impatience itched between his shoulder blades. He did mind sharing her with the sandbox. He didn't like saying it out loud, and on the one occasion he'd been drunk enough to mention it, Logan reminded him that she was still a Marine. They didn't really have the right to demand she be anything else.

Didn't stop a man from wanting, though.

"She can if she wants—and when she's ready, she will." It amazed Zach that Logan remained so easygoing about the situation. Like he didn't care what she decided as long as they were included in the decision.

"When's her next leave?" They should really change the subject, but like a dog with a bone, the need to hold on to her intensified. They talked with her nearly every other day, every day when she managed it. Sometimes for five minutes and sometimes an hour, depending on how much time she had.

But with no phone call in forty-eight hours, his gut churned with worry. He tried to keep a lid on it, but it boiled into everything he did.

Jace and Fin turned the curve on lap fifty, and Zach paused from throwing the ball to whistle. "Hit the showers, clean up. Be back here in the morning at oh-eight-hundred sharp." The practice field emptied out rapidly with Jace and Fin *walking* and thumping each other on the back in good humor.

Nothing like a little ass busting to make the heart grow fonder.

The tension in his neck wouldn't go away nor would the nagging sense of worry. He hated being on this side of the waiting game. It would be easier if he were there, in Afghanistan, with her.

Maybe.

His phone buzzed in his back pocket, and he waved Logan over. His shoulder burned from too many throws, and he'd have to ice it later. Tossing his friend the ball, he pulled his phone out. The number in the caller ID flashed familiar, and he thumbed it on to answer.

"Yo, Brody!" Lieutenant Brody Essex, the last member of their unit and one of the Captain's good friends, still served in the sandbox. A reassignment had sent his unit to Afghanistan two hundred clicks from Jazz. He'd checked in on her now and then to give Zach the news that yes, she was fine. "How goes the south side of hell?"

"Hot and crispy." The man's voice was tinny, echoing the distance between the calls. "Look, man, we just got word. The FET unit hit an IED in Bamyan. At least one serious injury. I don't know if it's her...."

The late afternoon sun turned icy cold. He froze, the sound of his heart like a ticking time bomb in his head.

"Zach?" Logan braced him with an arm.

"IED, Bamyan. A FET team was hit." He forced the words past the chokehold on his throat. The Marine inside him stood solid. Details first. Reaction later.

"I don't have any more details, but the news is going to hit stateside any minute. There were reporters there with one of the Army units. We're on our way now. Hang in there, buddy."

Brody's team was on their way. Brody's team specialized in recovery, alive or dead.

"Is it her?" Logan asked, the words a low growl.

"He didn't know. But she's in the field. She never says where she's going. Security." The words popped out, one at a time, like bullets being emptied from a clip. "She didn't call last night."

"Don't lose it." Logan's hand tightened on his shoulder. "We don't know anything yet."

She didn't call.

Zach stared at his phone, willing her to call.

It didn't ring.

Chapter Two

Zach paced a ten-step line back and forth in front of C Terminal's arrival gate for Dallas-Fort Worth International Airport. Logan stood to the side, arms behind his back. He waited in parade rest formation, except instead of a uniform he wore a black T-shirt tucked into well-worn jeans, and black biker boots—part of his physical therapy with the left one creating an almost cast-like effect for his ankle. He didn't necessarily need the damn things anymore, but he'd gotten used to wearing them.

The blue screens overhead blinked the baggage claim turnstile B for Flight 723 from Germany. But the carousel area sat empty and the international passengers hadn't exited from customs yet. On his umpteenth pass, Zach hissed a breath through his teeth. A vein throbbed in his forehead.

He is not doing well. Logan quashed the thought. Since Brody called about the accident, Zach was either planted in front of the television, on the phone with contacts in Washington, or calling the hospitals at Bagram and Ramstein. Jazz's injuries were severe. She'd lapsed into a coma for three endless days. They'd planned to fly out, but reports on her condition remained sketchy and every time she stabilized, they moved her to a new facility with specialized surgeons.

After thirty-two hours of surgery at Ramstein, she finally woke up. While Zach cajoled, coaxed, and bullied information out of the medical staff—fortunately they knew one of the Navy Corpsmen traveling with her—Logan took a different tactic.

He called her mother.

Mrs. Winters filled him in on Jazz's emotional state. It wasn't good. She didn't want to see them or speak to them. The rejection stung, but Logan understood. He'd been there. He hadn't wanted to see anyone either. It didn't keep Zach from annoying the hell out of him. Zach, who currently seemed intent on wearing a path through the hard floors of the airport with his incessant pacing, had stayed by his side through every agonizing hour of his dozen surgeries, skin grafts, and eventual therapy.

Not once, during that nightmare did his friend lose it, but he'd been there, seen the damage. He'd taken Logan's sour moods and anger without blinking. He'd be better when they saw Jazz.

Traumatic brain injury.

Those three little words would haunt Logan for the rest of his days. A remote detonated IED had burned and shredded the flesh on her arms and legs. The flash burns were the least of the doctors concerns. According to her mother, shrapnel from the IED cracked part of Jazz's skull, lacerated brain tissue and lead to swelling.

They removed a portion of skull cap until the swelling went down. She was in a war with seizures brought on by bleeding inside her brain. The doctors called them microseizures with partial physical paralysis. As soon as the doctors declared her fit for transport, they planned to send her back to the States for rehabilitation and recovery. When Mrs. Winters said those words, Logan told her about Mike's Place. He'd gotten the Doc and the Captain involved. Mrs. Winters agreed.

Fourteen days, ten hours and twenty-two minutes after

Brody's phone call, he and Zach waited to pick her up and transport her back to the Allen, Texas campus. Two Navy Corpsmen medics traveled with her and would remain with her until she was admitted to the newly finished medical wing and turned over to the Mike's Place physicians.

God, he wanted to hold her hand.

Zach's soft shoe swish ground to a halt, and Logan's spine jerked taut. The wheelchair rolled steadily toward them, carrying the most fragile woman he'd ever seen. Their Jazz was a physically vibrant, tough lady with an athletic build, warm tan, and sexy-as-fuck smile.

The woman in the wheelchair was ten shades of pale, despite the dress blues she wore. *Of course she flew in her uniform.* Logan wore his, even strapped to a back board and unable to stand. He'd insisted.

Pride fisted in his chest. Her silky black cap of pixie hair was completely obscured by the thick white bandages wrapped around her head. The closer she came, the louder Logan's heart pounded. Blue-black bruises smudged under her eyes. A single cut, mostly healed with fresh pink showing around the edges marred her cheek.

The uniform and the chair hid the rest of the damage. Logan would inspect every injury, every scar. He would know exactly what happened to her. Zach edged forward, practically vibrating with the need to push through the gates and greet her. An urge Logan shared, but the guarded look that washed over her tired face held him rooted to the spot.

He hated the hovering. He hated the pushy need of others who gave him sympathy, even when he'd needed it. In the two weeks since her injury, Zach seemed torn between a walking basket case and cold military precision. He had a platoon's worth of hovering in him. Logan steeled his soul. He'd let Zach hover for both of them.

Logan would treat her like the Marine she was. No matter how much he wanted to just pick her up and hold her until certain she really was alive.

The other passengers followed the wheelchair with its Navy escort. Surprisingly—or maybe not—they didn't crowd, push past, or try to go around. Normally those disembarking after a long flight were a chattering swarm. Not this crowd. It was quiet, respectful, and almost solemn.

He recognized the moment she saw them. Her slumped shoulders straightened, and she attempted to sit up in the chair. His heart ached at the slow, painful movements. It took enormous effort to keep his expression neutral. The wheelchair rolled through the gate, and Zach stepped up to meet her, blocking Logan's view. Her guardians stopped the wheelchair rather than run Zach over, and the man dropped down to his knees and collected her hands in his.

"Hey." That was it. One packed-to-the-brim-with-emotion word.

Logan's throat burned with a clog of feeling, but he swallowed it down. Time for his sorrow later. *Much later.*

Over a beer, when she was healthy and hardy and on her feet again.

"Hey." Jazz's husky voice never sounded so sweet. Logan unpeeled his feet from the floor and led with a hand open to the Corpsmen traveling with her—Corpsman and lieutenant, he amended as he took in their uniforms.

"Logan Cavanaugh."

The lieutenant shook his hand first. "Lieutenant Ambrose. You're our ride to Mike's Place?"

"Yes, sir. Welcome stateside, sir." Logan transferred his attention to the Corpsman.

"Corpsman Reade, sir." His grip was firm and brief, most of his attention on their patient.

"Our van is right outside. Airport security is holding it next to the door so we can load immediately." He glanced down. She held Zach's hand, but she stared at him. Pressure squeezed his chest. The faint, familiar scent of her—violets and vanilla—tickled his nose. One block-like stone rolled off his diaphragm. "Welcome home, sweetheart."

"Thank you." He earned two words and the shadow of a smile turned up the corners of her mouth. She paused, her expression frozen for the space of three heartbeats. Her hand in Zach's went slack.

The stone shoved against his chest again. "Jazz?"

The lieutenant dropped to his haunches and pressed two fingers against her throat. Logan fought the base urge to rip the man's arm from the socket and waited instead.

"What's wrong?" Zach leaned forward.

"Microseizure. Hang on." The lieutenant seemed unaware of the impending threat at his back. The words barely left the medic's mouth when Jazz's lips parted and she took in an audible breath. Her smile wavered and lines of tension knitted between her brows. "Hey, there, welcome back. That wasn't so bad this time."

This time. Bitter bile crawled up Logan's throat. *Seizures.*

They still didn't know the full extent of her brain injury. The research into that area seemed divided into two camps of *scary as shit* and *fuck me.*

"Let's go ahead and get out of these people's way." The lieutenant rubbed a comforting hand against her shoulder. Logan shifted, ready to intercept Zach as the blond man's eyes hardened. He recognized that look, and they didn't have time to interrogate the medics here. His gaze clashed with his best friend's and Zach nodded once. He pressed a kiss to Jazz's hand and circled the chair to take control of it.

She didn't need the Corpsman on station. They had her now.

Amazingly, the passengers had waited while they blocked the exit, and as Zach navigated the wheelchair around to leave, a small round of applause broke out. Jazz jerked with the barest flicker of a grimace and paled further, if that was possible. Logan nodded politely and gestured with a thumb for Zach to get her moving.

A little girl raced up and pressed a squished, well-worn teddy bear into Jazz's hands.

"Mr. Huggles wanted to say thank you." Two and half feet of precociousness beamed shyly with her offer.

Jazz stared at the child, her fingers slowly wrapping around the stuffed animal. She lifted it up until its worn face, sewn together with varying colors of thread, was eye level. "Thank you, Mr. Huggles." She kissed the bear's face and handed it back with all the gravity of a folded flag. "And thank you for bringing him to see me."

The child's face screwed up with concern. "He wants to know if the soldier will be okay."

"Marine." Logan, Zach and Jazz echoed each other, their deeper masculine voices swamping her feminine tones.

"I'm working on it." Jazz continued, meeting the girl's sweet concern. "I have to listen to my doctors, like you would your mom."

"Okay." The child hugged the brown bear to her chest. "I have to go now." She skipped off to a harried looking woman holding out her hand expectantly. The mother gave them a tight, sympathetic smile and ushered her daughter off.

Jazz sank back against the seat, eyes closed. Exhaustion filled the air around her.

"Let's go." Logan flanked the chair on one side, the lieutenant on the other with Zach guiding it, and the Corpsman in their wake. It was time to get the hell out of the airport. His heart drummed a march. A gentle touch brushed the back of his hand, and he closed his palm around her too cool, too fragile fingers. She squeezed with the barest of pressure.

Definitely time to take her home.

Ë

The ride back to Mike's Place passed uneventfully. Not that Jazz noticed much of the flat scenery or concrete highways. She fell asleep almost as soon as Logan lifted her out of the chair and into the van. The warmth of his ripped body pressed into hers, and she relaxed, letting go of the tension caging her chest in rebar. She hated being so helpless. She hated the conversations that came and went. The lieutenant had to remind her of his name constantly. If not for the uniform, she wouldn't know his rank.

The idea of forgetting Logan and Zach terrified her. How damaged was she? Seeing them come into focus as she wheeled down the concourse choked her. She knew them. She knew Logan. She knew every inch of his gorgeous body with its patchwork of scars. She knew Zach from his smile to the way she tickled his feet if she ran a toe against the bottom of them. She knew them.

The thought repeated itself in her mind as she drifted off and waited for her when she woke up. The blistering Texas heat smothered her as Zach eased her out of the van and into the god-be-damned chair. She cooperated, because the chair was the only way she'd obtained clearance to travel stateside.

Her admittance to the medical wing of Mike's Place sped past efficiently. Too many new faces came and went. The Corpsman and the lieutenant stayed with her through the process, reminding her constantly of where she was, repeating key phrases and information.

"Hey." Zach leaned against the doorway, all gorgeous polish in his T-shirt and jeans. His skin was a deep shade of golden brown. He belonged on the cover of a men's fashion magazine except his dazzling smile didn't quite reach his eyes.

She was so tired. "Hey."

"I should probably let you get some sleep." He walked into the room and dragged a chair over next to the bed. With one twist, he turned it around to straddle it and lay his arms on the back.

"Why?" Her thoughts seemed muddy.

"Because you're exhausted and you need to heal." His forehead furrowed into a frown.

"I mean, why are you in Afghanistan?" Why was she in the hospital? An iron spike of pain pounded behind her temple.

His swift inhale added to the strain on his face, but not the smile he pasted on. "You were injured in an explosion in Bamyan. You were airlifted to Bagram, and from Bagram to Ramstein. You're in Dallas, now."

"Oh." *We were at the university....* They were at the university doing what? She could see the room with the women, the younger girls with their bright garb and eager postures, their mothers dressed more sedately and maintaining a higher level of reserve. The light behind Zach's head began to kaleidoscope. A dozen different colors stretched out from the center until they filled her vision.

"How often does this happen?" Urgent frustration peppered Zach's words.

"Intermittent. It's increasing right now from the stress, give her a couple of days to sleep and recover from the trip...."

She didn't know that voice.

"If it wasn't safe for her to travel, why did they put her on the plane?" *Cold.* Logan never sounded so cold when he spoke to her. The alien tone rang warning bells in her mind.

"Mr. Cavanaugh, Mr. Evans, I understand that you're upset, but this is normal. She's experienced microseizures since she woke up from her coma. We've been monitoring them, and it's most likely part of the healing process." The third voice offered nothing but patience.

"Most likely?" Zach's question dripped with skepticism.

"Marines." But that patience seemed to wear thin. "You're worried. I understand, but bullying the medical staff will not help. Let us do our jobs. She remembers you, which is more than she can do for most of us. We have to keep reminding her. You may have to remind her for a while. Until then, get the hell out of the way so we can work."

"Don't go." She blinked the soft lens focus away from the edges of her vision. A hand squeezed hers, and she realized Logan held it. Medical personnel moved around her, and something cold pushed into her arm. The distraction pulled her attention, and she looked at it.

Her mottled-with-bruises-and-scrapes arm.

"What happened?"

Logan squatted down bringing his head level with hers. She didn't quite sigh with relief. Looking up hurt.

"You were in accident. You're back in the States. Zach and I are both here. We're not going anywhere. You need to sleep."

"What about the mission?" They were due in Bamyan. No, they were in Bamyan. She had to finish talking to the girls. Why were Zach and Logan in Afghanistan?

"You finished your mission. You're going to be okay. You're in Dallas with us. We've got this" Zach leaned in, his head nearly parallel with Logan's. "You need to sleep."

They were here.

Zach's hand covered Logan's on hers. Worried encouragement filled his dark blue eyes, flickering to doubt and concern and then back again. Logan's darker eyes remained steady and burned through her, just as it had when she'd first met him. If eyes were windows to the soul, his soul was boundless with determination and faith.

She didn't want to sleep. They were both with her. Both held her hand and the ice dripping into her arm didn't extinguish the fire spreading from their touch.

"What happened?"

⍓

She finally slept.

After the doctors added something to her IV bag and her unfocused gaze gradually closed, Zach continued to rub her cold, still fingers between his palms. She looked so damn delicate, a description she would scoff at if he confessed it to her. For two days, he and Logan shared vigil at her bedside, leaving one at a time, only long enough to shower and grab food. It was Logan's turn for a grub run, leaving Zach to wait and will her to wake back up.

Wake up and remember. He amended the mantra. She'd

woken a handful of times and always with the same questions. Why was she here? What happened? As fucked up as it was, he'd almost gotten used to it. They made sure to explain everything in easy to digest chunks. Most of the time she fell right back to sleep, but occasionally she drifted and asked the questions again.

Again.

Grit stung the corners of Zach's eyes. His body burned with the need for real sleep, but he shut that need away in a box. Trained to go forty-eight hours straight on a hard march through hostile territory, he could definitely handle a cushy assignment, sitting on his ass in the hospital room. Doctors and nurses came in regularly. They checked her vitals and the readouts on the machine. They wheeled her out for a CT scan—a hellaciously one-hour long scan—and nodded to themselves.

No one really seemed worried that she wasn't waking up. Not even Logan. Sure, he was tense and he didn't sleep any more than Zach did. But he didn't act anxious or concerned.

In the back of his mind, a little voice argued that wasn't fair. Logan cared about Jazz as much as Zach did. Hell, she was the only woman they ever talked about. He just couldn't do anything about her sleeping, so he didn't get bent. But it was the not being able to act that drove Zach crazy.

Her fingers flexed against his hand. He leaned forward. Her eyes fluttered, opening with such agonizing slowness. Her pink tongue flicked out as though trying to moisten her lips, and she coughed, the simplest, tiniest, dry-throated cough.

"Water?" He scooted the chair forward and scooped up the plastic cup with its bendy straw and held it to her lips. Barely focused, she sucked down a mouthful and then a second. He pulled it back when she would have taken a third and watched her throat convulse as she swallowed. Satisfied, he returned the straw for her to drink.

She lifted the IV-taped hand to push it away, and he set the cup to the side.

"Good afternoon."

"Hey," she said. He loved that little hey. It was a soft exhale of breath, simple and clean. Her coffee-with-cream stare warmed him. She smiled, her expression tentative. He waited for the questions. The *why she was here*, *what happened*, but she didn't say anything. Her pupils seemed normal, large, but they didn't seem to expand as they had during the seizures he'd witnessed.

The empty blankness that crept over her sexy face was the creepiest, most horrific thing he'd ever seen outside of battle.

"Jazz?" He rubbed her fingers against his cheek, trying to remind her that he was still there.

"I'm in a hospital."

The statement pushed a wave of relief through him. It was the first time she didn't ask a question. "Yes. You're in the States. You flew home a couple of days ago." He held his breath as her startled gaze alighted on him.

"Was I in a car accident?"

Shit.

"No, babe. There was an explosion in Afghanistan. You were injured. You've been in and out for the last couple of weeks, but they finally flew you home." He stroked her cheek gently. The fresh pink and rapidly fading scar on her too pale skin seemed to mock the rest of her injuries.

"My head hurts." An understatement, he was sure, but he kept that thought to himself. "Where's Logan?"

"He went to get food. He'll be back soon, so you need to stay awake for him." *He needs to get his ass back here.* Zach had to let go of her hand to tug his phone out, but he continued to caress her cheek. "I'm going to text him right now."

"Okay." Her lashes fluttered down and his texting finger froze. *C'mon, babe. Stay awake.* Sleep might be the best thing for her, but the utter stillness in her and lack of color in her cheeks haunted him. He needed the spitfire with her sassy red toenails and rapid-fire wit to make an appearance.

She focused on him again, and he finished typing the single word. *Awake.*

He hit send and set the phone down. "Outside of the headache, how are you doing?"

Her silence seemed to be the answer. She shook her head, almost warily. "I don't know. I think I felt better after twenty miles with a hundred-pound rucksack."

"Amen." A grin curled the corner of his mouth, one nearly as tentative as her head shake. "You look beautiful."

She snorted.

Relief swamped him. The tension knotting inside snapped.

"Zach?" She reached up to catch his hand, holding it to her cheek.

"Yeah, babe?"

"What happened?"

His heart stuttered.

"I mean, you said I'm back in the States. It had to be bad. What's the 4-1-1?"

He sucked in a lungful of oxygen. Her condition might not be the best subject.

Logan, however, took that decision right the hell out of his hands. "Skull fracture. Brain injury."

He turned a glare on his best friend. "Logan—"

"Don't." Jazz interrupted him before he went further, and squeezed his hand. "It's good. I need to know. My head is kind of full at the moment. Like there're too many thoughts in it, and it's kind of jumbled."

"I can imagine." Logan slid up next to the bed and perched near her feet. He dropped a couple of white bags onto the table over her hospital bed. "Burgers and fries, and you can have them if you want them."

Her mouth twitched and the first real smile he'd seen on her since Italy made an appearance. "Not really. Thank you."

Every moment she didn't slip back into the fugue seemed to lighten the weight on Zach's shoulders. "You hungry at all, babe?"

"No. It smells good. You two should eat. You look like crap."

Logan laughed. The tension bubbling in the room burst. Zach chuckled and snagged one of the bags as his stomach growled in agreement.

She tried to shift on the bed, and Zach shoved the food bag away to adjust the blankets. She froze in mid-motion.

"I wanted to sit up." The words were careful and wariness surged in her face.

"Carefully," Logan advised. Irritation scraped across Zach's nerves. She'd barely been awake five minutes, and Logan didn't care if she sat up. They didn't even know if she was allowed to sit up yet.

"Wasn't planning to hit the course today. Just sit up." Annoyance marched quietly beneath the words.

"Ease up, Zach. We're right here." Logan's advice added insult to aggravation, but he pushed it away. This wasn't the time or the place.

Logan pressed the bed control into her hand, guiding her finger to the button that would lift the head of the bed. She pressed down and held it. The bed inched up slowly until she still reclined but at more of a 120-degree angle than a 180.

"Better?" His best friend grabbed the white bag of food and pulled out a french fry. He munched it with all the nonchalance of sitting in a fast food restaurant rather than their girlfriend's hospital room.

"Yes. Actually. Though—" The words broke off and her gaze went flat. The pupil in her right eye swelled and seemed to engulf the brown.

"Dammit." Zach rounded on Logan. "We shouldn't have let her sit up."

"Maybe." The easy expression fled from Logan's face. He stared at her with a frown. "But we can't coddle her."

"She has a *brain injury*. We can coddle her."

"No, we can't. If she wants to push her limits, we have to let her."

Zach clenched his fist. His eyelid twitched.

"I missed you guys." Her voice punctured the anger weighing anchor in his belly. Zach jerked back around to find her looking back and forth between them.

"We missed you, too." Logan didn't miss a beat, even the strain seemed gone from his voice.

Zach couldn't quite mask his own reaction as easily and it pissed him off. He released his fist, somewhat surprised he'd considered slugging his best friend.

Not like it would be the first time.

"Yeah." Zach finally found his voice. And maybe his sense of humor. "We did, but you picked a helluva way to get a free ticket home."

Chapter Three

"Squeeze my hand." Reade, the nurse assigned to her care was in his late thirties, easygoing with a fast wit, and seemed more suited to combat than babysitting. He also worked with her on her initial physical therapy until she was ready to be signed over to the PT wing. His magic tricks alternated between the amusing and the irritating, either way, he got a reaction out of her. She was also sick to death of the tests.

"I am squeezing it." Two weeks in the hospital and three surgeries later, she achieved sitting up in bed on a regular basis. They still refused to let her walk, insisting on a wheelchair or rolling her to her appointments on a gurney. Flexing the fingers of her right hand around a ball made up her current assignment. She couldn't quite get her pinky and ring fingers to cooperate. Unlike the day before when it was her index finger and thumb.

Sweat beaded her forehead as she forced her trembling fingers into the correct position. They refused to stay there, releasing before she was ready. Tingles radiated up and down her arm, like a fallen electrical wire lashing back and forth in some bad action movie.

"Breathe. Inhale for four and focus, just grip the ball and

squeeze. One solid squeeze. Use all your fingers at once."

Did he think she wasn't doing it? Frustration swelled in her chest and pushed the oxygen from her lungs. She stared at her hand, willing it to cooperate. The ring finger locked down on the ball, but her pinky hovered, hesitating. The trembling shivering her skin spread up her wrist. Her hand spasmed.

The ball fell to the floor and rolled away.

"Fuck." She spit the word out. "Give it back to me."

Reade retrieved the ball, but rather than hand it back, he held onto it. "That's enough for one day. We're making great progress."

"No *we* aren't. I'm making shitty profits—" She grimaced and tried the word again. "Projects. Shit. Fuck. Damn a pussy cat."

Damn a pussy cat.

To the nurse's credit, Reade didn't smile. "Gunny, it takes time. You've had a total of seven surgeries, two of which were just to alleviate pressure on the brain. The doctors have ordered another CT scan tomorrow. But you are making progress."

Coddling didn't make her feel better. She flexed her fingers, but the pinky still refused to tuck into formation. Her left hand opened and closed. Her fingers wiggled responsively. Her right hand didn't. She needed her hand.

"Projects—prof—fuck—it's not enough." Some words were harder than others. At least she didn't speak in tongues. That led to another surgery and words like brain bleed being tossed around. Sweat slid down her neck. Her sheets would have to be changed again. It would help if they turned the air conditioning down, but her internal thermometer seemed to be broken. Squeezing a ball wasn't exertion, not like running uphill with fifty-pound pack on her back.

Reade covered her right hand with this, tucking the recalcitrant pinky where it belonged. "Gunny, you're making progress. You've had good recall the last two days. You can move your arms and legs. Gross motor control is responsive, fine motor control will return. You have to be patient."

Fuck patience. She scowled at him. "Give me the ball."

He sighed and pressed the ball into her hand. Sucking in a noisy breath, she latched her fingers around it. The quivers zinging up and down her arm intensified. Her forearm flexed. A brutal cramped seized her makeshift fist and her fingers locked in agony. She didn't whimper. She barely breathed, riding the wave of pain, until Reade plucked the ball away and began massaging her arm.

She wanted to prostate—prosaic—fuck—protest it. What the hell was wrong with *pr*-words? She didn't argue. She endured the strong thumb pressing into the cramp where the muscles bunched. The bruising pressure—at least *that* word was correct—radiated down into her hand until one by one, her fingers loosened. Her shoulders sagged with relief, and she drew in a shaky breath.

"Enough for today. You've got a visitor waiting, and I think you could use the break." He rubbed her arm, spreading the heat until only vague tremors remained of the episode.

A visitor. The spasm in her arm moved to her heart. It had to be Logan or Zach. They'd barely left her side, rotating in and out of her hospital room like the sexiest sentries on health patrol. Zach fussed, teasing her out of her black moods, while Logan gave her space and talked the business end of recovery. They were the perfect pair, coaxing and challenging her with absolute patience.

They repeated information to her tirelessly, but where Zach always seemed on the knife edge of worry, Logan maintained an easy stance. She loved them.

Both of them.

The pressure in her chest intensified. She always knew the day would come when she had to choose between them, but as impossible as it seemed, she needed both now. It wasn't fair or right. *Who fell in love with two men?* It would never work.

"Same time tomorrow, Gunny?" Reade gave her a pat and stood.

"Not going anywhere." The doctors refused to speculate on her recovery. A recovery measured in achievement, not minutes, hours, or even days. A swath of bandages still wrapped her head. She probably looked like Frankenstein's bride beneath the linen. At least she'd win the next bet on who had the worst scars.

The nurse opened the door and Logan filled the entranceway.

"Hey, Logan."

Masculine energy swarmed the room. Her body hummed appreciatively. Sweaty hospital gown and hairless condition aside, Logan never failed to make her feel like a woman. A woman who wanted very much to crawl out of the bed or— better yet—have him crawl into it.

"Reade. How's my gunny doing?" Logan may have been asking the nurse, but he never looked away from her.

"She's a Marine." Reade was Navy and his tone spoke volumes.

Logan grinned. "Yes, she is. See you later, man." He waved the nurse out the door and closed it behind him. Snagging the chair, he dragged it back over to her bedside. "So, how are you doing?"

"This sucks. I can't even make a fist." She held up her right hand, partially curled. The ache of the recent cramp twitched her fingertips as she tried to close it.

"What about your left hand?" His nonplussed response eased the aggravation in her soul. She curled that hand without any effort and brought the fist up parallel with her right. He nodded an acknowledgement. "Do you have feeling in the fingers on both?"

"Left feels fine. Tingles in the right."

"Then it's your nerves and we knew that might be an issue. PT will help. You have to be patient." Even though the scarred left side of his mouth didn't curl up with the rest of his grin, his easy tone carried rueful humor.

"It's fucking frustrating." At least fr-words weren't giving her shit. She leaned back against the pillows. She wanted a shower. She wanted out of this room. She wanted on her feet and walking. She wanted her brain to cooperate.

"Yep and bitching only helps a little." Logan caught her right hand, interlacing his fingers between hers and massaging them slowly. "But I might have a solution to at least one of your problems."

Her womb clenched. Did that solution include getting laid? Her nipples tightened at the very thought, but Logan wasn't looking at her body. Well, not precisely. He swept his glance down to her legs and back to her face.

"What's the solution?"

"How about we go outside for a little while?"

Next to sex, that was the best offer he could have made. She sat forward in a rush and the room wavered sickeningly. Her cheeks puffed with the three hard breaths she took, but she forced the nausea down. She needed out of that room, and her body could shut the hell up long enough to get her out of here.

Logan strode over to the door and pulled it open, retrieving a wheelchair outside and backing it into the room. Her heart sank. If only he didn't have to push her around like some damn invalid.

"It's the wheelchair or nothing." He didn't look at her.

"Fine." He didn't deserve her grumpiness, but disappointment rode hard on the bitch seat of irritation with herself, with him, with the whole damn situation.

He flipped her blankets back, revealing her chicken legs. The pale limbs lacked their usual muscle tone or definition. The bruises from the explosion were gone, but one jagged pink scar wrapped around her left calf and halfway across the shin. She didn't even remember the stitches from it, but it was an ugly little bastard. She started to edge her legs to the side of the bed, but Logan slid his arm underneath her knees and wrapped another around her back.

She barely had time to soak in the enjoyment of his touch

before he set her down in the chair. The room spun in a full one-eighty before righting itself again. Logan knelt next to the chair and pressed his hand against her bare leg.

"Breathe through it." The warmth of his grip on her thigh gave her another focus, and she latched onto it. Gradually the swimming sensation in her head eased up, and she gave a shaky laugh. "Better?"

"Yeah. I'm okay. Whew. So where do we get to go?" She forced lightness into her tone. "If it's another test, I'm going to be pissed at the bait and switch."

"I thought a stroll around the quad would be good for you, and your doctor agreed. We have to stick close to the hospital wing, but there's a great shady spot along the walking path we can take a break at." He dragged the blanket off her bed and tucked it around her legs. It couldn't possibly be cold enough outside to need it, but she didn't care.

She was getting the hell out of the sterile white room with its neutral décor and standard furniture. Cradling her right hand in her left, she tipped her head back to look up at Logan. "Thank you."

"You're welcome." He bent down and brushed her mouth with the barest whisper of a kiss. Her heart mimed a fist pump at the casual affection. It was the closest to a real kiss he'd given her since she woke up in Texas. "Now, eyes front, Marine. So you don't get sick."

"I'd rather look at you."

"Yeah?" The right side of his mouth inched up. "So would you rather do that in the hospital or outside?"

"Oh, outside. Definitely outside." She leaned back into the chair, gazing ahead, as ordered, and controlled the urge to cheer as he wheeled her out of the room, down the hall, and past the nurses' station. Reade glanced up from his paperwork. Her left fist clenched. He'd better not stop them. The Corpsman waved them on with an easy grin, but she didn't let go of her breath until they reached the end of the hallway and the automatic doors hummed open. A breeze of hot air licked her face as Logan pushed her outside.

The sun dazzled her and she squinted against the brightness.

"Want sunglasses?" His baritone stroked her ears. She closed her eyes and lifted her face to the sun.

"Nope. Just walk." She couldn't begin to describe how great the blistering heat felt on her skin. A sluggish breeze moved the humid air around, carrying the scent of green grass, fresh mulch, and the distant sound of laughter. Peeling her eyelids open, she squinted at the trees they strolled toward. They promised shade, but she almost didn't want to go back into the dark.

Too much of her recent past had been swallowed by darkness, and she could barely piece together the slivers of memory from the explosion, much less her time in the different hospitals. She didn't remember Bagram at all. Ramstein returned to her in the vaguest little fragments. Most of her memories came from Mike's Place—well, inside the hospital wing of Mike's Place. She hadn't actually seen outside beyond a glimpse here or there through windows as she'd been wheeled from one place to another.

"Doing okay?" They plunged into the shade beneath the first line of trees. The warning headache pressing against the back of her eyes receded.

"Oh, yeah."

The wheelchair stopped and Logan circled around to squat in front of her. He was dressed in his customary T-shirt and jeans. The white was a stark contrast to his tanned skin while the circular collar didn't hide the march of puckered skin down the left side of his neck. His entire left side was a mottle of burn damage, souvenirs earned following an IED flipping his vehicle in Iraq. She knew some of the details, but not all of them.

"Don't pull the Marine card. If there's a problem, you let me know. We're on shaky ground with the docs, but they agreed that getting you outside for a little R&R outweighed the risks."

She reached out to trace a trembling touch down his cheek to the damaged corner of his mouth. The rough ridges couldn't disguise the beautiful man underneath his battle scars. He leaned into her touch, rubbing against her fingers.

"Not pulling a Marine card. I like being out here. It doesn't smell like antiseptic." It smelled like sunshine, heat, green growth, and the barest hint of water as though the sprinklers had run. Or maybe it had rained? What did she know of the actual weather forecast?

"Good. James wants to come and see you."

She brushed her thumb against his lower lip. "Who's James?"

"Doc." The name didn't ring any bells nor did the designation.

"You don't think I have enough doctors?"

He caught her wandering thumb with his teeth and gave it a nip. "He's the doc I told you about, the one I work with."

The psychologist. She dropped her hand and leaned back. "I'm fine. I don't need a shrink."

"You're not fine. You're beautiful, stubborn, and glorious. But you're not fine. You've been through hell, and there's a lot more hell to go. James gets it. He can help you." He caught her hand when she would have folded it back into her lap. He stroked her palm, massaging relief with the heel of his hand. "You just started your PT. You're not even cleared for full scale PT until they finish your scans, and Neuro signs off."

Her grip on a ball was weak and that was just the beginning. Mutiny tightened her jaw. "I'll handle it."

"Yep. You will. But going through it without the right support is like going into a combat zone without intelligence."

"And that never happens." She snorted. In theatre, intelligence came in drips and drabs. It didn't—and often couldn't—take into account impulse decisions or snap judgments. Marines acted on the situation, in the moment, and often under fire. They planned when they could afford to and relied on their training, ingenuity, and fellow Marines for the rest.

"Jazz." Logan tightened his grip on her hand. "You need to talk to someone. You want to choose someone else, that's fine. But I trust James."

She wanted to dismiss the offer, brush it aside with the assurance that she would recover without all that. But four long weeks after the IED and she was doing well to remember who the doctors and nurses were. The seizures seemed to lessen but not the headaches. Her hand wouldn't cooperate.

She hadn't been allowed to try walking.

"Help me stand up." She wanted out of the damn chair.

"Not yet."

"Yes, yet. If you want me to meet with your Doc, you'll help me stand up." She dared him to tell her no again.

His jaw tightened and his gaze hardened. "You'll meet with the doc because that's what you need to do. Stop being st—" He swallowed the words.

"Stop being what? Stubborn? Stupid? Logan, I have been flat on my back or sitting in a bed for weeks. I don't even know if I *can* stand up, and no one seems willing to let me try. If I'm a wheelchair bound crip for the rest of my days, I *need* to know."

The words poured out like battery acid, burning through reason and patience. She couldn't close her hand. What if she never stood? What if she never walked? What the hell kind of life would she build that way?

What could she offer to either of the guys? She didn't want either one pitying her, and they deserved a lot more than a shattered woman, still hung up on how to choose between them. She had to be able to stand.

On her own two damn feet.

"Breathe."

"Stop fucking telling me to breathe. I know how to breathe. It's inhale and exhale." Only she panted in shallow, swift breaths. Her heart thudded a steady gallop in her chest, and the sweat beading her forehead dripped down her cheeks.

His fingers dug into her hands, shackling them in sharp, compressed pain. "I will when you calm your pulse back down."

He pressed his thumb against her wrist. Awareness punched through her haze of vision. He didn't grip only her hand. He held her fists. *Both of them, away from him.*

"It's a fist." She stared at her right hand, a bubble of hysterical laughter wobbling up. "I made a fist."

"I see that. Well done. You back with me now?" Logan's guarded words filled her with apprehension.

The day hadn't seemed to change. The sun still shone brightly on the sidewalks beyond their shady escape. Birds chirped overhead. A squirrel scrabbled down into the grass, completely ignoring them on its quest for whatever the hell squirrels looked for when they ran around. She still sat in the wheelchair, but her right leg was out on the ground, and Logan had her body blocked into the chair. He held her fists hostage, and she leaned forward, as though trying to rise.

Bile burned in her throat. "I think I just freaked out."

"Me, too. But your pulse is slowing and your respiration is easing. How's your head?" Despite the calm words, his tone remained wary.

"I'm sorry." Tears sheened across her vision and he wavered. Holy crap, she'd actually tried to hit him. She didn't remember moving forward or shoving her leg out. She didn't even remember clenching her fists. But his scar-free cheek boasted a red mark.

She *had* hit him.

She hadn't tried anything. She'd actually struck him. "I'm sorry."

"No problem. I'm going to let you go, and you're going to keep your ass in that chair. Got it?"

She nodded, mute. Horrifyingly, one of the tears leaked out. He let her go and she swiped at it. Her anger fled and she felt drained as exhaustion dragged her down.

She'd hit Logan.

"I'm really sorry."

He didn't respond, but scooped her out of the chair, blanket and all. Not the quick, transfer, bed-to-wheelchair hold he'd performed earlier. He wrapped his arms around her and hugged her. The pressure of his embrace provided such a profound relief, she burst into tears. They poured out of her, a throat-burning, sinus-stuffing sob.

She didn't want him to see her that way. She didn't want to do it. But she couldn't dam the tide once it began rolling out of her. She clung to him, turning her face into the juncture between his neck and shoulder. He ran his hand up and down her spine. He let her cry, supporting her weight like it was nothing. Her sobs finally tapered down to sniffling hiccups.

"When I woke up in the hospital, I didn't know what day it was." Logan confessed in a steady, even voice. "I didn't know where the hell I was. It came back to me in pieces, though. Jagged little shards of memory, each one cutting a slice in my soul. I screamed a lot. Because while I didn't know what the hell was happening or where I was, I did know I was in pain. Pain I don't know the words to describe."

His throat convulsed. He sucked in a deep breath, but he didn't put her down. She curled her fingers, even the stubborn ones, into his shirt.

"They gave me morphine, but that didn't make the pain stop—it just made me stop screaming. Broken bones are better than burns. The bones ache, but the burns never stop hurting. Every time I woke up, pain was the first thing I felt. Oblivion couldn't come fast or often enough. Surgery sucked, because every time they added another pin to my body, it was like I started burning all over again. But the worst part—" His voice choked. "The worst part was the loss of control. I pissed myself. I couldn't get myself out of the bed. I couldn't change position. I didn't have a damn thing to say about what happened to my body. I was a prisoner of war and my body was the camp. I get it, Jazz. I get wanting out and wanting to fight."

"Did you hit someone?" The low, strained voice was hers, but the cloud of tears and fear in it gave it an alien quality.

"Zach. I hit him twice. The first time he tried to help me get out of the bed. The second time when he wouldn't shut the fuck up at PT." Wry humor unfolded in his tone.

His continued to move his hand against her back, a soothing motion that amped up her other senses. She hurt. *All over.* Her body was one big, aching bruise. The white hot lances boring into her skull were worse.

"I didn't mean to freak out." The longer he held her, the safer and more secure she felt. It hurt. But it hurt in a good way. She wanted to run her fingers through his hair, kiss her way down his body, and show him how good it felt. But she wasn't even sure her legs would hold her up.

"I know." Logan's heart thumped a steady cadence beneath her ear. Little by little, the hard strength of his body pressed into hers. Despite the comforting nature of his hold, she felt the weight of his erect cock pressing through the denim. At least he wasn't completely turned off by her.

"I'm scared." She owed him a confession for a confession. "They keep saying TBI—traumatic brain injury—like it explains everything, but then they won't let me try to use my legs. My hand doesn't work right. Fuck, my memory doesn't work right."

"Not yet. But that's why you do the PT for the body and the MT for the brain." He sounded so damn sure.

"I need my brain fixed, not shrunk...." She'd already accepted the fact that she wasn't going back anytime soon. Other Marines would fill in where she left off. They would take care of Anoonseh and the other girls.

Logan's hip vibrated. A metallic tone, like a woodpecker hammering at high speed hummed. Images of the classroom filled her mind. Anoonseh's shy smile as she hurried down the hallway. She called *sar-jent* in broken English. The child hesitated and Jazz tugged off her helmet. The girls weren't always comfortable with their uniforms. She held out a sheet of paper with her version of 'what she wanted to be when she grew up' detailed on it. The vibration humming spiked through her mind. She grabbed Anoonseh and flung her into the room. Bright light enveloped her.

"Gunnery Sergeant Winters?" The light stabbed through her pupils.

Jazz blinked, turning her face away from it. Her head was so full and the light added to the pressure. "Stop." The word slurred.

"Easy, gunny. Can you tell me where you are?" *Who the fuck was asking that question?*

"Where's Anoonseh?" The stupid light cut through her vision again. Someone held her still.

"Answer him, Jazz. Do you know where you are?" Logan's muffled voice sounded behind her.

"I'm in Texas. At a hospital. Mike's Place. The fucking light hurts." Short sentences, but the assault by light stopped.

"Excellent, Gunny. Excellent. What's my name?" *Were they playing twenty questions?* She blinked away the blur bleeding at the edges of her vision and stared up at the lieutenant who'd swapped his uniform for some navy blue scrubs and a white lab coat.

"Lieutenant Masterson."

"Excellent." The Naval officer nodded. "Okay, no more field trips today, and we're going to get that CT scan now. You all the way back with us?"

"What happened to Anoonseh? Did I save her?"

"She's fine. Some bumps and bruises according to the on-scene guys, but no major injuries. You took care of her, Gunny." The doctor looked down at the chart in his hand. "I can send a request for an update if you like."

"Please." Memory trickled in. The hospital. The airport. The listing of her injuries. The walk with Logan.... "Logan?"

He shifted from behind her and filled her vision. "Right here, sweetheart."

"Did I freak out again?"

"Something like that. But they're going to run some more tests." He ran his knuckles down her cheek, a familiar caress.

"I am really starting to hate that word." Her insides twisted despite the rueful humor. Because what if they never figured it out and she kept losing pieces of herself?

How long before she lost herself entirely?

Chapter Four

"These are the anti-seizure meds. She needs to continue taking them as prescribed. I've marked everything with the timing. We're keeping her on the antibiotics, as well. We've broken the first week up into packets." Reade gestured to the thin white plastic wraps around groupings of pills. "We've also broken those down into the packets she needs to take. White for morning, blue for afternoon, red for evening, black for before bed. They should all be taken with food."

Zach listened, committing everything to memory. Three weeks after her final surgery—he crossed his fingers—the neurosurgeon signed off on releasing her from the hospital wing. Jazz needed to remain on campus. She had physical therapy every day, checkups with the neurologist, and appointments with James. He glanced at his watch. The first session with doc was scheduled in a couple of hours. Not a lot of time to get her home and settled in.

Home.

Reade pushed the pair of bags with her meds toward him. "You got this, Zach?"

"Yeah, I got it. Every six hours, take with food, get lots of rest."

"She will need the sleep. She's going to be a lot more tired than any of you realize. It's a big jump to leave the hospital. It's a bigger jump to start doing things for herself. If she's like every other Marine I've ever met, she'll start pushing the minute you walk out those doors. Don't let her overdo it. Falling isn't an option. Not yet." In the five weeks since she'd arrived back in the States, Reade served as her primary nurse and initial physical therapist.

"Been here before, Reade—with an even more stubborn Marine. We got this."

In the seven weeks since learning Jazz was the one injured, Zach didn't seem to sleep anymore. Not well, anyway. First it was the waiting for news, then waiting for her to come stateside, and lately it had been the wait to get the all clear from the neurosurgeon. Eight brain surgeries seemed an impossible number. Logan had gone through more, but those surgeries had rebuilt his bones.

The seizures worried him and so did the strokes. She suffered two of them in rapid succession. Every episode chipped away at the beautiful Marine, souring her hope and diminishing the gleam in her eyes. He wouldn't admit it out loud, and he sure as shit wouldn't say it to her, but the depression lurking in her soul leaked out.

She all but shoved them out the door most days. Pushing away, feigning sleep, and twice she picked fights just to piss him off. Yeah, he'd been there before. Logan's recovery took everything both of them had to survive, but they did it.

They and Jazz would survive this.

"All right, discharge papers are here. Her first PT is tomorrow morning. The Lieutenant wants to see her again on Friday." It was Tuesday morning, so three days neuro-assessment free would be a boon for her.

"Got it." He headed back toward her room. The sound of voices murmuring pressed through the door and he knocked twice.

"Yes?" Elizabeth Winters voice rose over that of her

daughter's. Jazz's mother had informed them of her planned visit. Weeks after her daughter threw her out after a seizure, her mother visited often, but she kept her distance.

He opened the door. "Ma'am. Jazz. I have the discharge papers and your meds. Logan took your things back to the apartment. We're ready to go when you are."

Jazz sat in the wheelchair she hated. She'd insisted on dressing and wore her uniform. Zach delivered it when he'd arrived, ironed and crisp. She still wore a crown of bandages, a blatant reminder of her numerous surgeries. He'd seen her without them immediately after one surgery. The missing hair barely fazed him. The neatly sutured lines were battle scars. The bore holes after her third surgery—those gave him pause.

"Thank you, Zachary." Elizabeth was a tall woman, like her daughter. Jazz inherited many of her mother's features, save for her eyes and her chin. Where the daughter possessed almost delicate features, her mother's jaw was longer, less rounded, and added to the image of her maturity. "Jasmine and I need a few more minutes if you don't mind."

He met Jazz's gaze. She nodded. She wanted the time, too. "Yes, ma'am. I'll be right outside when she's ready."

"Thank you." The women waited until he closed the door before they began talking. Their voices softened, he could hear snatches of the conversation, but not all. He tried to tune out the snippets. They deserved their privacy.

He leaned against the wall and glanced at his watch. His team had the day off, but they would be back on the practice field tomorrow morning. He would miss Jazz's first PT session. But that was Logan's territory, and even though he wasn't assigned specifically to her case, he would keep watch over her.

As if summoned by his thoughts, his best friend strode up the hallway toward him. Judging by the workout sweats he wore, he'd had a PT session of his own that morning, sessions he'd been missing while Jazz was in the hospital. His wet hair suggested he'd showered at the center and jogged right on over.

"She ready to go?" Logan asked by way of greeting.

"Discharged, but she's talking to her mom."

Her mother surprised Zach, although, with what he knew about Jazz, he shouldn't have been. She was a tough, resourceful woman who demanded answers in the form of the most polite questions. She didn't budge until she had the facts and then she pressed for more.

"Elizabeth is actually here? Jazz let her in?" Logan had never accepted Jazz's ousting of her mother. He'd made a point of keeping Elizabeth in the loop and encouraged her to be in the room.

"Yeah. She called her to let her know she was going to be discharged." Her mother's arrival concerned Zach some. Captain Dexter offered Elizabeth Winters an apartment on the campus. "She may want Jazz to stay with her."

"Jazz won't want that." Logan dismissed that concern with a wave of his hand, something he'd been doing a lot lately.

"You do realize that if she wants to stay with her mother, we're going to get cut out of the loop." Zach wanted her home, safe and sound, and they could take care to see she got her meds and to her appointments on time. He also wanted her where the bed was big enough that he could crawl in, tuck her against his side and know exactly where she was while he slept. He wanted her safe.

"Maybe. Elizabeth knows her daughter. Jazz doesn't want to be hovered over and her mom can't help it. She's a mom. But Jazz needs her support, so making up now is a good thing."

How the hell did Logan make it sound so blasé? Through the entire ordeal, he'd barely flinched at her prognosis, at her seizures, or her surgeries.

"Neither did you, but that didn't stop me from taking care of you. Her mom is here, she's local, and she has more say than we do." That fact sat squarely on the crux of his concern. He appreciated her mother's affections and needs, but he didn't want those to usurp his and Logan's place. Jazz needed to be protected, from herself if necessary. She needed to rest, to focus on her recovery, and not to put on a brave show for a worried parent.

"Man, when was the last time you slept?" Logan's concern barely penetrated the cloud of questions hammering to be heard in Zach's head.

She'd burrowed into his heart and claimed that battlefield without firing a shot. He'd never intended to fall for the Marine. He'd planned that date in Las Vegas to help Logan, to get him over the hurdle of impotence brought on by the trauma. He'd had a front row seat to the instant connection that flared between the pair—a connection that included him. That night the three of them spent together was one of the best of his life. The three days in Italy followed as nights two, three, and four.

"I'm fine. I'll sleep better when she's at the apartment." He repeated it like a mental mantra. From Brody's first phone call, he walked a razor thin wire between fury and fear. He preferred the anger. It kept him focused.

"Yeah, me, too. I checked the schedule. She's got Maxwell for first round PT. She's good. She'll push her."

"Jazz doesn't need to be pushed." The reply was almost automatic. They'd debated the issue for weeks. Logan insisted on setting a timetable. He'd been the one who encouraged Reade to get her physical therapy started before her surgeries were complete. He'd taken her out of the hospital for a walk that ended with her first stroke and brought in weights for her to work her arms because her right side remained weaker than the left.

"Yes, she does. Bringing in someone to do her nails isn't going to fix what's wrong." Two days ago, Logan found the manicurist Zach paid to visit, buffing Jazz's toenails. Reade pushed back her therapy for the day, so the woman could do her job. No matter Logan's opinion, Jazz relaxed more after that visit, a hell of a lot more.

"There's more to it than pushing her. She needed to feel pretty. Her nails had been growing and she kept snagging them. She wanted me to clip them all off, but the pampering helped." Her smile afterward was all the encouragement and thanks he needed. The grin stretched her full mouth wide and lit up her face in a way very little had since she'd woken up.

He'd learn how to do a damn pedicure himself if it could make her smile like that.

"She needs to feel whole. Pretty is like patching a bullet hole with a band-aid. She's fucking gorgeous."

Zach sighed. It was always so damn black or white with Logan. How quickly he forgot his own situation. His own shaken self confidence. He wore his scars with pride now, didn't flinch away from mirrors or the staring gazes of others.

Because of Jazz. Maybe his friend didn't see it, but Zach witnessed that struggle from the first moment to the last. Jazz changed Logan's world. She made him feel like a man again. Zach shifted against the wall, putting a lock on his temper. Maybe Logan couldn't see it. A dozen surgeries and weeks of rehabilitation had taken its toll on him.

They wouldn't let it take the same toll on Jazz. Reminding her of the good parts of being alive, of being a woman—of being their woman—would make a difference.

The door opened and Elizabeth Winters blew a kiss to her daughter as she stepped out. She closed the door behind her and stood in front of it. Zach straightened immediately from his lean on the wall, and Logan's shoulders stiffened next to him. The woman swept a look over both of them.

"Gentlemen. As her mother, what rank would you Marines assign to me?" Her navy slacks, white blouse, and navy colored jacket might have been business attire, but she wore an air of poise and authority they didn't dare ignore.

"General," they echoed each other.

"Excellent." She smiled a dangerous smile and focused on him, and Zach swore the weight of it pressed right against him. "In that case, my daughter insists that she would rather go home with you than have me take an apartment here despite Captain Dexter's generous offer."

His relief at that statement was short-lived.

"Now, that said, do not expect that I will be a stranger or that I won't be watching the two of you. She needs proper care, rest, and to get out of that wheelchair before it sucks the soul right out of her. You will look after *her* needs and not your own."

Zach nodded once. He agreed with that assessment. Logan nodded, too. It seemed they were on the same page.

"As far as I know, the doctors have not cleared her for sex. So no taking turns and absolutely no ménage shenanigans until her doctors give the okay."

Yeah, that's not uncomfortable. Zach cleared his throat. From the corner of his vision, he glimpsed Logan's half-grin. The man possessed a warped sense of humor.

"Are we clear?"

"Crystal." Zach hoped his face wasn't as red as it felt. Talking to her mother about sex, much less their *ménage shenanigans* was not high on his list of dinner topics, much less standing in the middle of a hospital hallway conversation.

"Elizabeth, we're one hundred and ten percent behind her recovery. We won't do anything to impede that. I give you my word." Logan extended his right hand and Elizabeth shook it, but Logan didn't let it go immediately. "You won't have anything to worry about."

Mrs. Winters smiled and patted his scarred cheek with maternal affection. "You're a sweet boy, Logan. But don't try to shovel horseshit at me. You're all Marines. My daughter wouldn't know how to take it easy if it kidnapped her with furred handcuffs and hot chocolate. But I will be watching— both of you." She glanced from Logan to Zach, including him in the warning. "Don't screw this up."

"Yes, ma'am." Logan released her hand, and Zach fought the urge to salute. Civilian or not, Elizabeth Winters understood a lot more than he'd given her credit for.

"Good luck, boys." The older woman adjusted the strap of her purse, and as she walked away, Zach swore she added, "You're going to need it."

He waited until she was down the hall and out of their direct line of sight. "Wow."

"No kidding." Logan laughed and pushed his way into the hospital room, Zach hot on his heels. Jazz stared at them moodily from the wheelchair. "Hey, sweetheart, you ready to get the hell out of here?"

"Yeah." She reached down and popped the lock on the chair's wheels. "But maybe my mother's right, maybe, I shouldn't impose on the two of you."

"What?" Zach skidded to a halt. "How are you imposing?"

"You've both got lives, jobs, responsibilities, and currently I'm a full-time job." The depression leaked into the open spaces between the words, no matter how strong her voice sounded.

"Correction, we *all* have lives. You're the prettiest and most interesting part of ours, so it's hardly an imposition." Logan glanced around the room. "Anything we forgot that you're going to need?"

"No." The word rode out on a long sigh. "Apparently I didn't pack much before I came home." The black humor did little to alleviate the doldrums in her voice. "Roxy boxed up my stuff, but it's probably headed back to the Navy Yard." Her home base before she went overseas.

"We can get it." Zach had connections. Connections he used to get information on her and to smooth the transfer of her care to Mike's Place rather than Bethesda or any other Naval hospital.

"It's not important." She waved off the offer. "Are we driving or walking?"

"Walking." Logan studied her with a frown. "We thought you'd enjoy being outside for a bit before the apartment."

"Excellent." She didn't wait for either of them before getting her chair going. In the last week, she'd started fighting against anyone pushing her chair. It killed Zach to watch the strain on her face. He stepped forward, but Logan's warning look stayed his hands. She needed her independence.

They fell into step on either side of her as she worked her way up the long hall toward the doors. The staff lined the hall. One by one they began applauding until the hallway echoed with their cheers. Jazz kept rolling, her attention fixed on the door, but there was the barest smile on her face. Even the patients in the rooms they passed added to the applause.

"Oorah, Gunny!"

Jazz paused to look sideways at the Marine sitting in his own wheelchair inside the room. His right leg was gone from the knee down. "Oorah, Marine. Don't get lazy because I'm out of here."

"Yes, sir." The Marine saluted, a salute she returned. The moodiness evaporated from her expression, replaced by pride.

Sucking in a quiet breath, she got the chair going again. Out in the sunshine, she squinted. "I don't suppose anyone brought sunglasses this time?"

Zach tugged his own out of his pocket and pressed them into her hands. She slid them into place and then touched the bandages on her head with a grimace.

"I should have my cover."

"When the bandages come off." Logan squeezed her shoulder.

"I can be Frankenstein's Marine." The humor was more bleak than black.

Zach's frown deepened. Maybe they should take her over to see James right then rather than head back to the apartment. He cut a look at Logan, but his friend walked with his gaze straight. The stiffness in his gait reminded him of Logan's own continued recovery.

"The apartment is two klicks."

"Got it." Jazz nodded, her expression grim, but determined. Two klicks could be covered in nine minutes at a decent pace.

Zach's palms itched to take control of the wheelchair, but he fought the urge to reach for it. As though reading his mind, Logan gave him a nod. The hardass may have wanted her to do it, but it wasn't as easy to watch her exertions, particularly when the path began a slight incline.

Thirty minutes later, they arrived at their second-floor apartment. When Jazz stared at the steps, Logan and Zach each took a side of the chair and hoisted it, carrying it up and into the landing.

"Your first appointment with James is in a little over an hour. Do you want to grab a shower?" Logan unlocked the door and she relinquished control of the wheels long enough to let them guide the wheelchair inside. Maybe they should have requested a ground floor place. But he and Logan both liked the extension that put them on the corner with no one living below.

"Would love one, but I can't get the bandages wet." She motioned to the white linen wrapped tightly around her head.

"That's why God invented the PX and shower caps." He'd already cleaned the store out so they had plenty for cover along with feminine products and three different kinds of soap. He'd bought shampoo, too, but Logan grabbed it out of the bag and hid it in the kitchen.

Her expression froze. "Seriously?"

Logan picked up her bag from by the door where they'd delivered it earlier. Clean uniforms, workout gear, and some casual items her mom delivered to the hospital. "Yep. You can't stand, we know that. But one of us can take a shower with you and keep you on your feet. We have to go slow, no more than ten minutes. But that's long enough to shower. Sponge baths suck."

"Then, hell yes, I want to shower." For the first time that day, she sounded like herself.

Zach grinned. He'd fought against the idea, but Logan was right. A shower was a luxury people forgot until they weren't allowed to take one. Long patrols were like that—spot washes and dry shampoo.

"Who...?" She lifted her gaze, meeting each of theirs for the first time since they arrived at the apartment.

"Zach won that coin toss. I'm getting the grub ready. Shower, some food, and then we'll head over to see James." Logan's easy tone carried no hint of jealousy or envy. Zach wasn't sure he would have felt the same way. On the other hand, knowing the way Logan liked to push, they'd probably end up having sex in the shower. His cock stirred at the idea, and he tamped down the urge. He'd kept that need under rigid control. She needed his support, his care, and his attention—not his lust.

Not yet anyway.

"Do you mind a lift back to the shower to save some time?" Zach itched to get his hands on her, to hold her. Stripping her down for the shower would be torture, but the kind of torture he relished. He wanted a good look at the damage.

She hesitated briefly and finally nodded. "Probably not a bad idea. Not sure the wheels will like the carpet."

He winced inwardly. They needed to get some plastic desk mats and lay them down to create a better surface for the wheels. He shared a look with Logan. They'd get it taken care of. With as much care as he could manage, Zach scooped her out of the chair and cradled her close. The antiseptic smell of the hospital didn't disguise the distinctly feminine scent of her—it wasn't perfume or lotion, just Jazz. Her arms wrapped around his neck. Relief suckerpunched him. She was in his arms.

Finally.

All Marine. All woman. All theirs.

☙

The rich patchouli she associated with Zach filled her nose as he lifted her from the chair. He'd been so damn stingy with his touches, holding her hand or caressing her cheek, but refusing to touch her otherwise. Resentment flared when he made the offer to carry her to the shower, but the fact that he had to touch her to carry her beat back the annoyance.

Logan waved them off. "Ten minutes and we'll have burgers ready to go."

"Got it!" Zach pivoted and marched down the hallway. They passed two open doors—the guy's bedrooms, which on passing glance seemed to be carbon copies of each other right down to the made beds with their tight folds and tucked in sheets. The last door at the end of the hallway opened into a larger room. Like the two they passed, it was decorated with minimal frill.

But the bed was larger.

A lot larger.

A thrill skated from her belly up to her nipples and down again. Zach didn't even look at the bed, unfortunately. He carried her through into the bathroom and settled her down on the closed toilet lid. "Need the facilities before we start?"

"No, I don't want to—" The sentence cut off as she stared at the mirror over the sink on the opposite wall. Her heart sank. The woman staring back at her wasn't her. It couldn't be. Her face was nearly ashen, the tan buried under paleness. Her eyes were too large for her face, smudged with black shadows beneath them. Her hair was gone, replaced by the white bandages like a skullcap.

The room shrank around her and as hard as she tried to peel her attention away from the mirror, she couldn't help staring. She hadn't seen herself, not in all the weeks in the hospital. She'd been limited to bed pans and sponge baths with the occasional trip to the bathroom. The tiny mirror in that room was never her focus.

"Hey." Zach squatted down in front of her. He caught her face in his hands and turned her to face him. "Look at me."

"Who is that?" She tugged her gaze away, she didn't want to see herself in the mirror, but it was as though she couldn't stop.

"That's my beautiful Marine who walked into hell and back out again. Show her some respect." His hands tightened on her cheeks, and she obeyed him this time. His bright blue eyes shone with conviction.

"Zach, I'm not beautiful. Not even close." She'd never really given a damn about being beautiful or even being girly. She was a damn good Marine—or she had been. Before. *What the hell am I now?*

"Yes, you are." He punctuated the sentence by slanting his mouth over hers. She froze under the kiss, but he didn't let her pull away. He teased the seam of her lips with his tongue until they parted. The slow, sweet invasion derailed her self-pity. The taste of him rolled over her. The gentle caress of his fingers against her face sent electricity zinging through her. She gripped his shirt, half to push him away, half to pull him closer and slid forward on the seat.

He nibbled at her lower lip, grazing it with his teeth and slowly broke the contact. Forehead resting lightly against his, she stared into his eyes. He was so damn pretty it hurt to look at him. The blond hair, tan skin, chiseled features, and sexy-as-sin grin belonged on a magazine cover or a surfer, not a Marine. He was almost too good-looking to be a Marine.

He was kind, generous to a fault, and funny as hell. Her heart squeezed.

"We're getting naked and we're taking a shower now. You okay with that?"

No, she wasn't okay with that. She didn't want him to look at the horror show that made up the stranger-in-the-mirror's body. She didn't want to shower. She wanted to go back to Las Vegas—to be the woman strutting down the hallway and into the hotel room with the sexiest pair of Marines she'd ever had the pleasure to meet.

But that wasn't happening.

So she nodded and refused to look as he helped her unbutton the uniform.

Chapter Five

Zach's arm locked around her midsection, holding her upright and supported against him. The first spray of the overhead jets striking her skin stung. The warm water didn't hurt, but it almost seemed her skin was too tight, too new, too unused to the way the water hit it to be comfortable.

"Too hot? Too cold?" His breath tickled her ear and his body pressed intimately against her, her back to his chest, his hips to her bottom. The weight of his cock prodding her lightly surprised her, but she couldn't quite grasp all the sensory data assaulting her. The water drowned it out—like static noise of the flesh.

"It's fine." She raised her hand, forcing it up the shower stream so the water pounded against her hand and washed down her arm. She fumbled for the words to describe it. "I want to put my face in."

Obeying the request, Zach's hand flattened against her belly, and he nudged her legs with his. The half-slide, half-pushed step forward shoved her into the waterfall. The water sluiced over her face and she closed her eyes. It reminded her of rain. Lifting her chin, she pushed her face further into the downpour. It stroked her eyelids, smoothed over her cheeks, and trickled down her neck.

Laughter quivered in her belly and rolled up. The elated sound echoed against the tiled walls. Zach eased her backward from the overflow. She wanted to lock her legs, to resist, but her muscles didn't obey her. The left leg did, but the right leg didn't. Her knees were rubbery, and the world rolled from side to side as though she rode the tilt-a-whirl.

"Shhh." His whisper soothed the ache clawing inside to get out. "We're gonna do some soap and then back under."

"Don't talk to me like I'm a child." The words lacked real heat.

"Trust me, sweetheart. I don't think you're child." As if to emphasize the point, he rubbed a washcloth across her chest. The fabric rasped over her nipples and the tips pebbled expectantly. A current of need buzzed through her, swarming from her breasts down to her sex and back up again. Her legs buckled and she sagged back against him. Zach's arm stroked up her belly and caught her just below her breasts. The contrast of his warm tan against her mottled paleness cramped the desire flooding her limbs.

She bit the inside of her lip and tasted blood, but she managed to stifle the moan climbing up her throat. He continued his torment, lathering her chest and shoulders. Just when she became accustomed to the spicy storm heating her breasts, he soaped a path between her legs. An almost foreign bliss buzzed up from her sex and heat flooded downward. Fighting to catch her breath, she slapped a palm against the tiled wall.

The arm holding her up banded like steel around her middle. She would not fall. He wouldn't let her. Her fingers curled. The hard cotton rasped against her sex, stroked the inside of her thighs in silken, hot, soapy fashion and rasped against her clit. *Too much.*

The orgasm rolled her under. The vanity lights rainbowed as though a kaleidoscope through the water. The buzz of pleasure centered at her core and zinged through her body. Her muscles spasmed and released. She came too fiercely. She opened her mouth to scream and all that escaped was a long moan. Her nails scraped at the tile, fighting for purchase, to hold the line against the torrent.

Zach murmured to her, but she could barely understand the words. Another caress against her clit and she rode the roller coaster again. Tears leaked from the corners of her eyes, and her heart slammed into her ribs. It was too much. The cloth fell away and his hand cupped her sex. She wanted to clamp down on him, ached to feel the pressure of his fingers—or better his cock—tunneling into her.

Her damn muscles refused to cooperate. Her recalcitrant thighs quivered, failing her control. She couldn't grind against his hand or urge him inside. His fingers rested against her clit, neither stroking nor removing the pressure.

"Shh, sweetheart. You're way too sensitive and I'm sorry, I didn't realize how much." Her head lay back against his shoulder. The heel of his hand moved in slow circular motions, wringing another womb-clenching climax from her. Her knees buckled and the only barrier keeping her upright was the hard body wrapped around hers.

His fingers abandoned her sex and ran up and down her body. Sluicing off the soap, she realized belatedly. He shut the water off and carried her out of the shower. Thankfully, he didn't seem to mind her boneless lack of cooperation. He settled her on a towel laid over the toilet lid and once she sat, he went to work with a second towel, drying her off efficiently. His cock thrust outward, a raging hard on bobbing between his legs.

Son of a bitch, she got off and he was the one hurting right now. She caught one of his hands on the upward stroke. "Zach...."

He pulled his hand away and gave her a stern look. "No touching, sweetheart. I'm already reminding myself that you aren't up for this yet, and it's taking everything I have to not pick you up and take you right against the wall."

A quiver rippled through her belly and wet heat soaked her

sex. They used to do that. He loved walls. Hell, he loved any hard surface. For all his beauty and his charm, he loved it rough and wild.

"God, babe...don't look at me like that." The words were nearly a groan, and he wrapped the towel around her and shuffled away before she touched him. He stuck his head out the door and into the bedroom. "Logan!"

The man in question appeared within seconds, his gaze snapping sharply from Zach to her. "What's wrong?"

"Help her get dressed so I don't do something I regret later."

No matter how much she tried to tell herself that wasn't a rejection, the request stung. Jazz folded her arms in front of the towel and squirmed back, not that the low counter tops really hid her emaciated form.

"I got this, go walk it off." Logan didn't have to make the offer twice. Zach practically fled the bathroom. All business, Logan scooped her up, towel and all from the toilet seat and carried her into the bedroom. "You want your uniform back on or something else?"

"MARPATs." The word shouldn't be that hard to say.

Logan set her on the bed and unzipped her bag. "I'll unpack this when we get back from seeing James."

Fantastic—from orgasm to rejection to the head shrinker—her day was complete. Logan carried back a Marine green T-shirt, bra, clean underwear, and her MARPATs. Her fingers went to her bare neck and swallowed the tears clogging her throat. "Where are my tags?"

"They kept taking you back in for surgery and had to remove them." He tugged the chain out from under his own shirt and her heart squeezed. Her tags hung on the chain. He draped the them around her neck and the metal, still warm from his body, tingled against her skin. "Better?"

Strangely enough, she did feel better. Not quite trusting herself to speak, she nodded once.

"Okay, babe. Let's get you dressed and fed. Clock's

ticking."

଼

The psychologist turned out to be a nice-looking guy in his thirties. While his hair wasn't clipped to standard, it was neat and matched his business dress appearance. She'd eaten the burger Logan sat in front of her and tried not to notice when Zach joined them—still damp from his second shower and dressed once more. She lied that the burger was good, ate at least half of it. It sat inside her stomach like a lead weight. The stilted conversation ended quickly enough because they had to get her to the appointment.

James dismissed her escort much to their chagrin and wheeled her into his office behind closed doors. For ten minutes, she'd sat there, saying nothing—aware of the doctor's assessment.

The silence weighed on her.

"How does this work?" They were the first words she managed since their introduction.

"We talk. We don't talk. It can work a variety of ways. How do you want it to work?" An easy-sounding answer to a not-so-easy question. She turned her attention to the great picture window overlooking a landscaped courtyard populated by trees and flowering plants.

"I don't know. I prefer rules and regulations. Procedure." All of which was true. She specialized in making things happen. She managed men, supplies, and intelligence.

"Makes sense, you're a Gunnery Sergeant. You're used to managing situations and people."

Except that she couldn't manage at the moment. The joke was on her. She clenched her left hand into a fist. Her right hand ignored her save for a rude twitch of her middle finger as though flipping herself the bird.

"Yes." It was a better answer than the one screaming inside her head.

"Procedurally speaking, therapy is about what you need.

105

So if you want to make a list of conditions or topics, we can focus on those one at a time." He made it sound so simple. She shivered. The room was too cold.

"I don't know what's relevant." Lists required assignment of priority and value.

"Everything is relevant."

She laughed, the humorless sound harsh to her ears. Was desiring two men relevant to being blown up? Did her body's lack of cooperation have a priority over the desire to fuck them? She had no hair, she barely looked like a woman, and her life as Marine could very well be over. So what use would they ever have for a broken Marine?

What use do I have?

"Too general?" James leaned back against his chair, one leg crossed over the other. He appeared utterly normal, comfortable almost, as though willing to sit there all day.

"Non-specific requirements lead to non-specific responses."

"Fair enough. You were upset when you arrived, and you appeared relieved when the guys left. Why?"

Well, that was specific.

I had several orgasms, and Zach ran away. I guess being turned on by Frankenstein's Marine isn't as appealing in fact as it is in theory. "I'm just tired."

"Gunny, do us both a favor. If you don't want to answer, say so. Lying doesn't help."

Anger surged up to pound against the back of her eyes. She recognized the completely irrational response, but the torrent seized her like a ragdoll and carried away her reason. "Don't call me a liar. I may not understand what the fuck my brain is doing or why my brain is doing it to me, but I am tired. Really fucking tired."

"Because lying in a hospital bed is work and so is rolling around in that wheelchair."

Was he for real? "I was injured."

"You were injured. But that was weeks ago. What's your

excuse now?"

Fury ballooned in her chest, pinching her heart and squeezing her lungs. "My brain isn't working. You think I want to be stuck in that bed? You think I want to be in this wheelchair?"

She tried to shove her right leg out, but it only twitched and slid off the foot rest. Pain dug hard fingers into her thigh, the muscle twisting brutally. "I'd walk the fuck out the door right now if I could."

"And that pisses you off." The mild understatement didn't deflate her frustration.

"Of course it pisses me off. I forget things. They repeat information to me over and over. For a week they taped sticky notes to the tray in my room so I remembered where I was. Why I was here...what happened."

"Why are you here?"

"Because some fucker planted an IED in a university and tried to blow me up."

"Tried or succeeded?" The mild tone continued to hammer at her.

"Succeeded or I'd still be in theatre." *I wouldn't be broken. I wouldn't be here. I wouldn't have had Zach's hands on me or Logan's dog tags around my neck.* Pain spasmed in her chest.

"But he didn't succeed." The doc's voice dragged her back to the room.

"What?"

"The guy who planted the IED wanted to kill you. Presumably he wanted to kill a lot of someones—maybe even the little girl you saved. But he didn't succeed. You're alive."

She snorted. "What kind of a life am I going to have? I'm like the walking dead. Scratch that, rolling dead."

"Marine, you've had eight surgeries. You had shrapnel that impacted your skull and cracked your cranium, impacting the brain beneath. You nearly died on the table, but you didn't. A lot of people would still be in the hospital, but you've left the room behind. You've got a long road in front of you, but don't forget just how far you've traveled already." James' expression mirrored his words, equal parts stern reprimand and gentle sympathy. "You want a checklist for your recovery, make one. Set your goals. You have an entire company here to help you make it happen."

"I can't ask them to do it. It's not fair."

"I'm sorry. You can't ask who to do what?" He zeroed in on her outburst.

"I can't ask Zach and Logan to wait or to wonder, or to even be there when and if I can ever choose. And if I choose, how do I do that? How do I stick one of them with a cripple? Wouldn't it just be easier to walk—well, when I can—walk away?" Her head hurt. Where the hell had that come from? "Sorry, this isn't about my personal lack of morals. We were talking about the IED."

"Jasmine, we're here to discuss you. Everything is relevant. What choice are you sweating about?"

The interesting phrase touched a chord of awareness. Sweat slicked her arms and soaked through her shirt. Despite the icy chill in the room, droplets of perspiration rolled down her face. Her hands trembled. Hell, she didn't even do therapy right. "It's not important."

"I think it's important. It sounds like it's troubling as much as what happened in Afghanistan...."

"I don't want to talk about it...not with you. Not with them. I have to focus on getting back on my feet. I have to be me again." He needed to let it go, let her have some shred of her dignity.

"Tell me about the explosion."

Thank you."I don't really remember it. A buzz. Running. Bright light. Then I was in Germany."

"What was your assignment?"

Jazz pinched the bridge of her nose. Her eyes burned, but she stemmed the tears before they fell. "My FET team presented to a group of local girls and their mothers about educational opportunities. We've been gaining momentum in the outlying villages, particularly those where the women had to run everything anyway. City women are harder to reach, but the task is to bring those villagers in, set them up, and create an environment that local women will want to participate in."

"What was your role in this assignment? Specifically?" His pencil scratched on the notepad in front of him.

"I was the closer. Roxy, she engaged, handled opening arguments, and revved up the crowd. Stormer delivered the facts, the statistics, and set the playing field. I made it emotional by encouraging them to apply the information and the ideals to their own personal goals. If I hooked one girl, she usually brought two or three with her."

James took more notes. "How did you know who to hook?"

"I watched them. You can tell a lot from body language, how a person leans forward, or withdraws. Similarly eyes are great storytellers. The girl who wants to know more, squints. As though in a personal struggle between culture and curiosity. The one who showed the most interest was the one I went after." The tension in her shoulders eased.

"What is your success rate?"

"Twenty-eight percent—up from twenty-four last month."

"How often do you hold those meetings?"

"We tried for weekly. We moved the locations frequently, to make it easier for those traveling, and we spent the intervening week visiting villages with information about the meetings." She was thirsty.

"Are you in love with Logan and Zach?"

"Yes."

The word escaped before she fully acknowledged the question. Her lungs squeezed. Jerking her gaze up, she focused on the doc, but he simply added another note to his legal pad.

James stared at her steadily. "Why, is that a problem for you?"

The air in her lungs whooshed out. "Because I can't be in

love with two men."

"Is that a regulation somewhere?" He lifted a brow.

"Yes." Cold prickled her neck.

"Where?"

"I...." She trailed off. It was a rule. *One man. One woman.* A ménage was a fantasy.

"Gunny?"

"It's just an impossible situation. I don't want to talk about it." She looked back at the windows, hands fisting together in her lap.

"Why did you join the FET team?"

ಬ

"I hate being out here." Zach drummed a cadence against his thigh, pacing back and forth. They had fifteen minutes more before her session ended. His stomach tied in knots. He'd damn near fucked her in the shower and again when he had her out of it. His job involved taking care of her, not himself. But all he thought about during his second shower was how wet she'd been against his fingers, how responsive to the lightest touch. The provocative allure of her moan as she came apart for him echoed in his ears.

His balls ached thinking about it. He'd palmed his dick in the shower, jerked off to the thought of her. But thrusting into his own grip didn't come close to sheathing his cock in her pussy or feeling it clench around him.

"Dude, sit the fuck down." Logan sprawled on one of the sofas. He propped his bad leg up on a table and leaned his head back, eyes closed.

"How can you relax?"

"I didn't get the boner in the shower." The dry comment didn't help. "And pacing out here doesn't make the time go faster—it just irritates the shit out of you."

"Says the master of waiting." He couldn't help the frustration. How Logan compartmentalized the bad shit never failed to amaze—or annoy—him.

"Yep. You learn patience when you have to rely on someone else to wipe your ass. Walking's a real bitch of a lesson too. Sit down." Logan didn't look up.

Zach flung himself down in a chair, the leather seat bouncing once with his weight. "I almost screwed up."

"You didn't hurt her. Hell, an orgasm probably felt damn good at this point."

"That's not the point. It was a shower, but...."

"But she's entirely fuckable, and you aren't the only one who can't wait. Just give yourself a break, man." Logan sat forward and slid his leg off the table where it thumped to the floor. "Seriously. I'm not entirely sorry I lost that coin toss because I want to work my way over every inch of her body. Carrying her is hard enough. Naked...."

They both sighed.

"We're so fucked." Zach chuckled.

"Yep." Logan bobbed his head once. "We have to keep our focus on the prize. Get her better."

"Yeah." Who was he kidding? He was ready to jack off again thinking about all the things he shouldn't do until she was better. His cock strained against the front of his jeans. *Think about something else.* "Who's handling her PT?"

"Phillips." Logan grimaced. "Captain ordered me off her case directly. Too much personal involvement. But I'll be there. Moral support, ass kicking, whatever she needs."

"Cool."

The clock inched forward.

"Your kids got a game this weekend?"

"Three. Regional series against Plano."

"Fin and Jace got it together yet?"

The short stop and outfielder were getting on Zach's last nerve. The kids worked well enough in practice, but in their last three games they'd crashed together and fumbled with more errors than first time little leaguers.

"May have to move Fin from the outfield to first base. Jace

thinks he has to beat Fin to the ball for some ass backward reason." He should be out there working with them right now, but he'd turned the team over to Damon for the day. The chef may specialize in spicy foods, but he knew his baseball. Zach was where he wanted to be.

Mostly.

Considering where he really wanted to be was nibbling on the inside of Jasmine's thighs and licking up the sweet cream of her pleasure as she orgasmed into his mouth. His cock hurt.

Baseball just wasn't enough to get his mind off her.

"We need a plan, Logan."

"We have a plan." His best friend gave him a stern look. "We keep our schedules rotating so one of us is always with her. She does her PT. She sees Doc. She makes her neuro visits. We help her put herself back together."

"Okay, that covers about two or three hours of her day, what about the rest of it?" On their one long weekend, they watched a lot of movies and had a lot more sex. Sex wasn't on the approved list of activities and there were only so many movies a body could watch.

"Man, she's gonna sleep. A lot, maybe even more than in the hospital. Physical therapy is going to take it out of her." In that, Logan was the expert.

Zach didn't remember Logan sleeping all the time, but once he'd been discharged from the hospital, he'd spent hours at the apartment while Zach worked. "Maybe I can take her to the field for practice some days. You know, get her out. Set her up in the shade."

"Maybe. Does she even like baseball?"

The two stared at each other and Zach frowned. He had no idea. "Guess we'll find out."

"Twenty says she's an Astros fan." Logan preferred the National teams and their refusal to allow designated hitters.

"Rangers." Jazz grew up near the Metroplex. She had to be a Rangers fan.

"Fifty says she hates the Cowboys." Logan grinned. The

man was a Redskins fan through and through.

"Done." They shook on it and the door opened. The laughter drained out of Zach as Jazz eased her chair out the door. Exhaustion etched every pale line of her face. He stood still while she struggled.

"I'll see you tomorrow, Gunny." The Doc's expression remained neutral, betraying nothing of the session. "Logan, got a minute?"

"Sure." Logan circled the coffee table, caressing Jazz's cheek before following the Doc back into his office and closing the door.

"Hey." Zach strangled the rioting urges in his body. "How you doing?"

"Tired. I wanted to try and go for another walk—roll—whatever." She smacked her hand lightly against the chair. A glimmer of tears flashed in her eyes, but she blinked so rapidly and looked away that he wasn't sure.

"Sounds like a plan. You want to wait for Logan or let him catch up?" Her refusal to meet his gaze hurt, but what the hell did he expect when he'd practically mauled her in the shower.

"We can wait." She pulled her upper lip between her teeth. Her right hand drummed a cadence against the chair arm. "Is there water?"

"Yeah." He closed the distance between them and tugged a pack off the back of her chair. They'd stuffed it with energy bars, water bottles, and a change of clothes—anything she might need while on the move.

She stared at the bag in confusion. "Did you tell me that was there?"

He shook his head slowly. "No. I was going to or maybe Logan was, but I don't think we mentioned it."

"Oh." Relief crawled over her face.

"Oh, shit. Babe, I'm sorry. No, you didn't forget it. We just wanted to make sure if you needed something, you had it." He pulled a bottle of water out, and twisted the cap off before handing it to her.

She stared at the bottle cap and her expression emptied. She glanced down at the bottle and lifted it to drink. It shook a little in her hand, sloshing the liquid onto her already sweat-dampened shirt. He fisted the bottle cap and the hard plastic dug into his palm. The door opened behind her.

Logan's face was tight with worry following his chat with Doc. He stared at Jazz before clearing his throat. "We ready to go?"

"Yes." Her response echoed his right down to the dregs of relief. He lifted his brows in silent question while slinging the pack over his shoulder. Jazz kept her water bottle.

Logan shook his head at Zach and mouthed, "Later."

Fuck. What's wrong now?

Chapter Six

*L*ogan watched Phillips lean on Jazz's right leg, forcing her to push him away to strengthen it. Her face was a mask of concentration. Tension tightened the lines around her mouth and squinted the corners of her eyes. Three weeks of the absolute same routine—physical therapy in the morning from five a.m. 'til nine a.m, her appointment with James ten until eleven, lunch 'til twelve. Then she napped or at least retreated to her room for the rest of the afternoon.

They were losing her. She'd pulled back on every front.

Her right leg extended, shoving Phillips upward, and the therapist's legs began to slide. The grueling control on Jazz's face gave way to satisfaction.

"Oorah, Gunny!" Phillips broke into applause that echoed around the room.

Belatedly, Logan saw that he wasn't the only one staring at the strength contest between his woman and her therapist. The gym played host to any number of recovering servicemen and women. Her right leg hadn't cooperated with her since the first of two strokes she'd suffered after arriving home. In the beginning, Logan put it down to the trauma and the brain surgeries. But her neurologist and neurosurgeons both confirmed that strokes were partially responsible for the loss of feeling and control in her arm and leg.

Jazz sat up, refusing Phillips' assisting hand. A green baseball cap covered the spiky growth of her hair—a hat she insisted on wearing at all times. Whether it was the need to be in uniform or what, she refused any civilian clothes whatsoever, relying on her MARPATs and her standard Marine workout gear. She wrapped the colors around herself like a barrier against the world.

He understood that desire, maybe better than she realized. But the sturdier she built the barrier, the more she shoved them to the outside. Both of them. That morning had been the last straw. Her cutting dismissal of Zach, the phone call to Phillips and request for a lift to physical therapy effectively shut Logan out as well. His jaw tightened.

Last. Fucking. Straw. It was time for a come-to-Logan meeting.

James' words from his last session echoed in the back of his mind. "You know, you can talk about this. In fact, I think all three of you should." He didn't mind Doc talking about Jazz, even though James refused to, more often than not, beyond initially telling him she would need a prescription for antidepressants. He didn't want to talk to James about Jazz— he wanted to talk to Jazz.

And today, we are going to talk. You and me, babe, he told her silently.

She fixed the hat back over her head. In a smooth, practiced motion, she worked her way to her feet, resting her hand steadily on the locked down wheelchair. She hated the device, despite the limited mobility it granted her, but walking still eluded her press for recovery.

Sweat soaked her green T-shirt. A faint tan warmed her pale skin. Muscle tone began to fill her legs back out. She'd put back on ten of the thirty pounds she lost during her hospitalization. She needed to gain more to return to the curves he was familiar with, but he didn't care if she was as skinny as a chicken wing. If she was healthy enough to push him away....

She was healthy enough for the push back.

Phillips nodded to him. Their session was done. Tamping down his innate desire to get his hands on her, Logan marched across the room and took hold of her chair. "Good job. You in?"

She glanced up at him, wariness shuttering her expression. He gave her an easy grin, the same grin he gave her after every session. She wanted to retreat? No way in hell would he let her do that.

"Yeah, I'm in." Her guarded tone warned him she wasn't interested in being pushed around. *Good, maybe it means she's ready to push back.*

He unlocked the wheels, gave Phillips a wave, and guided the chair out of the building. He was silent all the way to the apartment. At the foot of the stairs, he locked the chair and lifted her out of it. She weighed next to nothing. Mutiny pinched her lips, and he allowed the barest hint of a smile.

He strode down the landing, aware of every feminine curve pressing into his side. The frailty she'd exhibited during her initial weeks hardened during her workouts and physical therapy. She may not have mastered walking yet, but she was close.

He would be damned if she was going to just walk away from them.

"What's wrong with you?" she asked. The question dropped into the oppressive silence clouding their trip to the door. He balanced her and unlocked the apartment. The maneuver might have been tough a month before, but practice made perfect.

He could handle anything, even while carrying her.

"Hmm?"

Normally he paused for lunch. Not today. She'd resisted showers with either of them after that first day. Her statement that she preferred her privacy in the bath smelled of a need for independence. He understood the body shyness, but they should never have backed off on them. That was Zach's plan and he'd insisted. Zach wanted to coddle her, to keep her safe, and make her feel safe. But that wasn't working either. If anything, the more they catered to her need to push the away, the further she retreated.

Retreat's over.

"You seem pissed." The faintest quaver of doubt crept into her words, and she wasn't 'not looking' at him anymore.

Yes, Gunny. Pay attention to the terrain. This is about to be a bumpy ride. He shrugged a shoulder and pushed open his bedroom door with a foot. He closed it the same way. No swift escape for her. She stiffened in his arms and he ignored it. Setting her down on the bed, he rolled his head from side to side, battening down the hatches on his temper. This wasn't about anger or rejection. It wasn't about withdrawing from the front lines or pressing the advantage.

He tossed his keys onto the dresser and made quick work of stripping out of his clothes. Once upon a time, he wouldn't have done that right in front of her. The thick scars from the fire in the vehicle mottled his skin from his face to his thigh. His left leg wasn't a pretty picture either, crisscrossed with surgical scars. But she never shied away from his body, never made him feel like less of a man—not even when she had Zach to compare him to.

"Get naked. You need a shower."

"I don't want to take a shower." She stared at him. Her expression tensed, and she focused on his face, but her gaze kept drifting down to his body. Her nipples strained against the front of her shirt, clearly outlined by the material. He didn't smile, but her obvious reaction to him eased the worry gnawing inside his gut.

"But I do want one. I want to take one with you. I want to hold you. I want to touch you. I want to fuck you." Logan didn't mince the words. He could dress them up, call it making love, but the unbearable tension in his balls didn't want pretty words. "I want to have hot, wet, blow-your-mind sex." He didn't tack on the *like we used, too.*

Desire flared in her hazel eyes. "I—"

"You?" He knelt down, pressing right up into her space, flattening his palms on the bed on either side of her. "You what?"

"Logan." She shifted her weight, not quite squirming, but the troubled cloud darkening her expression stabbed at him. *What was she afraid of?*

"I'm right here, babe." He caught her wrist and pressed her hand to his chest. "You can touch me. You can feel me. You can see me."

"It's not that." She glanced to where her hand rested on him. Her right hand. The one she struggled with and cursed about. Her fingers curled against his skin, the barest of friction, but it sent need raging through his blood.

"Talk to me, babe. We can't fix it if we don't know what the problem is." He laid bare the core of his anger. She wasn't talking to them. She wasn't telling them what nibbled away at the inside of her soul. Logan would face any battle, he'd take on any enemy, but he couldn't fight what she would not allow him to see.

"What if the problem is you?" The lack of conviction in the words eased the injury they offered.

He settled his weight onto his right knee, the left didn't like the pressure still—even on the thick padding of the carpet. "If the problem is me, then I really can't fix it if I don't know the source."

"I'm not that woman anymore. The one who walked into that hotel room in Vegas. I—" She tugged her hand away. Rubbing it against her face, she jarred the hat loose and jerked to secure it.

Eyes narrowing, he pushed her hands away and swept the hat off. Her wince stabbed him. "No, you're not *that* woman anymore. *That* woman was a stranger, one I damn near missed out on meeting because I wasn't me anymore. I hadn't figured out how to really be me after the surgeries. I'm not a handsome man—"

"Yes, you are." Her swift defense demanded a kiss, but he fought that urge, silently promising he'd reward it later.

"I'm not. But it wasn't the physical scars, Jazz. It's the scars on the inside, the ones no one else can see." She needed a push, a very hard push. It would hurt like hell if it backfired, but he was tired of the distance she kept trying to put between them. Watching her struggle and fight as though she were alone exhausted him. He'd never left a man behind, and he sure as shit wasn't about to start now.

Starting at her cheek, he stroked his fingers up and down the side of her face. "You've been through hell. I know that. I'd like to say I know exactly what you feel, but I don't. I know what I think you're feeling. But I'm not inside that beautiful head of yours."

Her unspoken denial of the compliment flared in her eyes. He knew it would. She didn't recognize the woman in the mirror. She saw the damage, not the strength. She saw the horror, not the joy. She saw the pain, not the survival. Steeled against the consequences, he touched the stubble where her hair should be. They'd shaved all of it off. The stitches were healed, but the fresh pink scars betrayed the recent damage.

The flinch warned him away, but he wasn't about to shy from a battle that had to be won. If she truly believed that her scars made her unattractive, it was up to him to prove otherwise. He rose to his feet. Shifting to slide sideways onto the bed next to her, he pressed his lips to the first scar he saw. The stubble was rough and soft, almost downy in spots. He traced the long scar where they'd removed the shrapnel. She froze against him. Her right hand clutched at the air, but she didn't push him away.

"You know what the scariest thing has been for me?" A circular scar dimpled the back of her head. "It wasn't the news, the hospital stay, or the surgeries." He stretched around her, punctuating each word with another soft kiss. It was truly the first time he'd been able to see the scars. She covered up whenever they were in the room and resisted their presence when the neurosurgeon or other physician checked on her.

He waited her out until her silence cracked under a damp sniffle. "What was the worst part for you?"

"The part where you pushed me—both of us—away." He whispered the last against her ear. "If you don't want to have sex. Fine. If you think you're uglier for whatever reason. Fine. But sweetheart, that's not what I see and that's not what I feel. I just want to hold you, to be there for you, and to face this down with you."

The last made him a bit of a liar. It definitely wasn't fine if she didn't want to have sex, but he could wait and would wait, if that was what she wanted. He lifted his head, backing off enough to see her face.

"I want *you*." Warts and all. He couldn't make that any clearer.

"This is so messed up." She wrinkled her nose and laughter hinted around the edges of her watery smile. "I'm messed up. Why would anyone want that? You guys have lives—had them—before you got stuck with me."

Unfortunately, no matter how much she believed that statement, it only pissed him off. He closed the distance and captured her mouth in a kiss that was equal parts affection and anger. Cupping her face in his hands, he gave her no room to evade or escape. In this, if nothing else, she would accept his leadership. She might be lost in the woods and uncertain of how desirable she was, but in this he demanded submission. He ran his tongue along the seam of her lips, requesting access. Her mouth softened, opened, and welcomed him.

A long, low groan of need thrummed through him. He'd kept his distance, pressed her only about what she needed to do physically to recover, watched her medication, and hounded her about her appointments. He'd done everything except show her with his body how important she was to him.

An issue he planned to rectify immediately. Her nails scraped his scalp, tugging him closer. The kiss was far from gentle. The contact threatened to do him in, his body screamed readiness at the flood of heat, the wash of hunger. He fought to hold steady, to pour his need and desire into the contact.

When he finally lifted his head, she stared at him, slack-jawed and panting. Her nipples pressed eagerly against her shirt. Her hands held onto his head and her eyes were wide, liquid. She trembled, but it wasn't weakness he sensed at all. But need.

"Damn." Zach's low whistle sliced through the tension. Jazz didn't quite jump, but a flush of red stained her face and she jerked to look at the Marine leaning against the now open bedroom door. "That's hot."

"In or out, but you're killing the mood." Logan didn't spare his best friend a look. The guilt and confusion edging into her wanton expression begged his attention.

"I am heading out to pick up some things. You ladies need anything?" Zach's words said he was leaving, his tone asked to stay. Logan didn't care, but he wasn't as certain about Jazz.

"Sweetheart?" He gave her a nudge. It was her call, if she wanted ménage shenanigans, then that's what they'd give her.

"No. I mean...no, thank you." She stole another look at Zach.

"'Kay. You two have fun." The door's soft thump indicated he left.

"Did it bother you that he walked in?" Logan wanted to understand what was going on inside her head. She was still dressed. He was buck-ass naked. "It was just a kiss."

"It shouldn't...I mean, we've all...well, I've been with both of you, right?" Was she asking him or telling him?

"It's not a matter of would or should, it's a matter of does." His balls ached, but he shoved their demands aside.

"Most men are more possessive...they don't want to be excluded." She began to lean back, but Logan still held her face. He gave her a half an inch. No more. He liked feeling her pressed against him.

"I am possessive as hell. You ever look at another guy the way you look at us and you may find his continued good health in serious question."

"But not Zach?" Her brow furrowed. Was she really asking this question? Hadn't the way they met set those rules into motion in the first place?

"There's no jealousy with us." He massaged her face. The frown and confusion needed to go. Zach was his brother, his best friend, and the lighter hearted side of his soul. It had taken him years to understand they were flip sides of the same coin. "We don't need it, we don't compete, and we never have."

"So you could walk in on the two of us having sex and it wouldn't bother you?" For whatever reason, she needed these questions answered.

"Nope. I might want to join in—I might even watch, especially if his hairy ass isn't on top." He grinned. "But it's just as hot to watch you getting off...he got you off in the shower a few weeks ago—"

Realization slammed into him.

"Babe? Is that what this is about? You got off with Zach in the shower and worried that it would upset me?"

She glanced down to stare fixedly at his chest. "Yes and no. That night in Vegas—it was amazing. It was everything I wanted it to be and more."

Hell yeah, it had been. He'd walked in that hotel room with negative expectations and walked back out a changed and proud man.

"I never asked myself what came after. I went to Afghanistan. I saw you in Germany. I saw Zach in Italy. Logan—how the hell is this supposed to work?" The hesitancy in her voice flattened to crisp anxiety. "You can't marry two men. You can't choose between them. If I have sex with you, I have to have sex with him and then it gets even more complicated. You throw in the fact that I'm a cripple, and I'm leaving the two of you to decide who gets to babysit me."

"Whoa." Logan held up a hand. He had to get a grip on his

temper. "Who the hell said you had to do anything you didn't want to do? Having sex with either of us doesn't mean a damn thing unless you want it to mean something. But let's be clear, you call yourself a cripple again and I'll kick your ass."

Her jaw tightened and flexed. Heat flared in her eyes— good, he'd pissed her off.

"I'm a mess, Logan. I still can't walk...I'm working on getting my hand to cooperate, and my last assessment recommended six months to a year. A year. They're recommending that I accept a permanent disability discharge."

"That sucks." And it deflated his anger. Permanent disability would earn her benefits and an honorable discharge from the service. No more trips to Afghanistan. No more duty in the line of fire. No more doing the job she enjoyed. It sucked. But sucking had benefits, too. "It's not a final decision. It's a recommendation."

His disability discharge was final. He couldn't pass the physical now, even if he tried. He could do most of it, but the uneven ground would throw him. It sucked. But he accepted it, although the news was a bitter pill and left an acrid taste in the mouth.

He imagined it was the same for her. No wonder she withdrew from them and painted herself a cripple. He tugged her close and kissed her, hard and fierce. Heat swelled between them and when her hands roamed down his body, he groaned.

Too long without the feeling of her naked flesh against his, and finally, she seemed to be tired of it, too. He pulled away only long enough to help her strip. Fortunately, he knew where every button and zipper lay. He scooted her further up the bed and stretched out next to her. Light years of progress in seconds and Logan lifted his head to look at the nightstand, long enough to check that the condoms were there.

God, he hoped he would need them.

She traced the line of his jaw with her fingertips. The

caress skated down his neck to his chest. He refused to remain still while she explored, tracing the line of her throat to her chest. He slid a hand over her breast and it peaked, stabbing his palm. She was a woman who demanded pleasure, even now. He skimmed the palm back and forth across the nipple. It darkened to a deep rosy shade, straining desperately. She arched up and he met her stormy gaze.

"Logan?" Need strained her voice.

"Yeah, babe?"

She sucked in a breath. Her pink lips were swollen from his kisses. "I want to have that really hot, wet, sex now."

Hallelujah.

He caressed lower, cupping her sex and sealing her lips with a kiss at the same time. She rolled toward him, lifting her hips to drive against his hand. He'd like to fuck her senseless, but as much as he needed to exert control over her body—he maintained it over his. His cock already beaded with pre-cum and shivers of pleasure tightened his balls until he thought they might explode.

He took his time, stroking a finger up and down along the delicate slit. He swirled his thumb against her clit. She bucked, riding his touch. Zach said she'd been wildly sensitive in the shower. Now he had his first opportunity to taste her responsiveness.

Already pathetically close to coming on the bed cover, he focused his attention on her. Her kiss grew demanding, her tongue twining with his as though fighting to taste all of him. He teased her pussy until he slipped a finger inside her slick channel. Her heels dug into the mattress and her legs spread.

"More." She broke the kiss, gasping. Pleasure spiked in her dark tone. He was selfish. He wanted her to come for him and he wanted to watch. She wrapped her fingers around his cock and he damn near went cross-eyed. "Logan, I don't want to play—I want you to fuck me. Give it to me...please."

She did not have to make that request twice. Groaning, he rolled over her on the bed and grabbed for the condoms, the box flying as he pulled one out. Seconds later he settled the sheath into place and lifted her hips. One thrust and he would be inside her. He shook with need seething beneath the reins of his control.

She wrapped her legs around him. He grinned slowly. She pressed her heels into the backs of his thighs. He braced with his good arm. He didn't want to squash her.

"Fuck me, damn it." She dug her fingers into his arms and he laughed. Glaring, she tightened her legs as though trying to force him inside, but he held steady, the tip of his cock barely teasing her entrance.

"Do you see what you're doing, babe?"

"What?" Agitation and curiosity warred in her eyes and she squeezed him with her thighs.

"You're using your legs." He slid his cock inside her, amazed as hell at this powerful woman with her ability to turn his insides to mush. He'd never thought of himself as a romantic before, but he could learn. He eased in, inch-by-inch, because she was so fucking tight. Her pussy clenched around him, pulsing as he buried his cock to the hilt. God, he wanted to stay there forever.

But his impatient little Marine arched up into him, and he took her mouth in a kiss. He tried to be tender, but she wasn't having any of that. He rocked into her, stroking his free hand up and down her body. He wanted it to be good for her. She looked up at him, gaze dark and stormy with pleasure. She held onto his back, urging him deeper.

Her orgasm came quick and she cried out against his mouth. He let go of his control and the world unraveled to the feeling of her pussy clenching him, the friction of her flesh rubbing on his, and his cock jerked as he came.

Chapter Seven

Regret arrived with the dawn. Her heart hung heavy in her chest, echoing the thud of her conscience's outrage that she'd given into desire and had sex—although sleeping with her head pillowed against Logan's chest was the best night's rest she'd had since waking in the hospital. Pushing up onto an elbow, she studied his sleeping face. He looked so relaxed, one arm tucked behind his head, the other flung out and wrapped around her.

It's never going to work. No one lives in a full-time ménage. This is a fling—a fucking fantastic fling—but life doesn't give a woman two perfect men other than to make her choose. Carefully, she stretched her arms and began to sit up. Three weeks ago, she'd needed help to get that far. But her arm cooperated more often than not even if the tremors in her hand continued.

The tangled sheets shoved away easily when she scooted to the edge of the bed. Her movements were careful, in part to gauge how well her leg would behave, and in part to not wake Logan up. The carpet rasped against the bottom of her feet and she curled her toes, like she'd practiced in physical therapy.

All ten curled. All ten released. *Oorah!* Pressing one fist against the bed, she rose, feet flat against the floor.

"What are you doing?" The husky tone in his sleepy voice caressed her senses.

"Going to pee."

The bed dipped as he levered up. "Nudge me. I'll get you in there."

"No." She shoved off the bed and stood. Her legs trembled, a hundred pins and needles rolled up from the bottoms of her feet to prickle along her flesh. Logan bounced into her periphery, one arm out as though to catch her and she glared at him. "I got this."

"Jazz...you're still not up to this in PT. Let me help." His hand brushed her arm, and she pulled away, stumbling to the side before catching her balance against the wall. Walking shouldn't be that damn hard.

"If I can wrap my legs around your waist, I can walk on them. I can still do this even if my brain is fuzzy on the details. I need to pee...I just fucked you, I don't need you to wipe my ass or treat me like a bedridden invalid." He didn't deserve the harsh tone and she softened it. "Logan—I need to do this myself. You want to hover and catch me if I fall, fine. But don't unless I am falling."

He withdrew his hand, his expression shuttering. She saw the hurt but refused to be moved by it. The last thing she wanted to do was injure him, but she'd tried to tell him what was wrong the night before and he didn't get it. Or maybe she sucked at explaining it. It was hard to say that she needed to choose between them when they acted like it was okay for her to be with both.

But for how long? It's okay now. But six months from now? A year from now? No. Better to cut the loss before it kills us. Unfortunately, they both held fast to her heart and no matter how insane it seemed, she was in love with both of them. *Focus. Walk to the bathroom. Take a piss. Walk back. It's not hard. You used to do it all the time.*

"All right." He acquiesced, almost too easily.

Not one to look the gift horse in the mouth, she put one foot in front of the other and used a hand against the wall to maintain her balance. The walk to the bathroom wasn't more than a dozen feet—but it stretched out ahead of her like miles.

She avoided the mirror as she stepped inside and made her way to the toilet. There was no shame in flattening her hand on the counter as she turned to sit down.

"Open or closed?" Logan stood right next to the door.

"Closed. Please."

"You got it." The door shut and she sighed. It didn't take long to finish.

"I'm standing up again." The door swung inward at her words. She did it. She walked to the bathroom and used it alone. Her muscles trembled but she didn't care. Success tasted sweet. "Would you mind taking a shower with me?"

His guarded expression softened. "I'd love to."

Thirty minutes later, she walked out of the bedroom with one hand braced on Logan's arm for balance. She was pushing it. Phillips would have her head on a platter, but she didn't care. She hated that damn wheelchair. The only way to get out of it was to walk steadily.

The enticing scent of bacon and coffee drifted from the kitchen. They followed the inviting smell through the living room, and her heart did a little fist bump with her ribs as Zach caught sight of her.

"Well, check you out." He grinned. Pride gleamed in his blue eyes and his white teeth provided a startling contrast for his tan skin. He appeared relaxed, flipping pancakes while bacon sizzled on another pan. "How's it feel?"

"Crazy good." She flashed a smile up at Logan, tickled when the right corner of his mouth turned up and he winked. "Not perfect. Yet. But it will be."

"Hungry?" The loaded subtext in Zach's question teased a fresh wave of heat in her belly. He looked good enough to eat.

"Starving." she promised.

"Then carb up, Marine. You have a lot to do today." He

pointed them toward the table where steam rose from the coffee mugs and a dozen pieces of fresh toast waited.

"Yes, sir." She wrinkled her nose and began the slow walk over, seeming to get steadier with every step. But the faint trembling warned her not to take longer strides. Logan shifted his grip to her elbow, steadying her as she sat. She glanced up at him and smiled. "Thank you."

He slid his fingers around the back of her neck and tipped her head back. His lips glided over hers and his tongue invaded. Hunger flooded through her. The kiss demanded and gave in the same breath. When he lifted his head, the heat in his eyes warmed her. "You did great."

She blew out a heady exhale and glanced to find Zach's hot gaze on them, amusement and desire battling for dominance in his expression. Her nipples tightened at the want in his face and she curled her toes inside her workout shoes. His expression promised they would be naked before the day was over. Her growling stomach interrupted and heat rushed up to her face.

"I'm starving." She pressed out another deep breath and reached for the coffee cup. She could do this. She would eat and enjoy them and figure this out.

ଔ

"She doesn't think it can work." Logan grabbed a bag of sand from the trunk and carried it easily over his right shoulder. On and off rain over the last three days had done a number on the pitcher's mound. It surprised Zach when Logan volunteered to help rather than stay with Jazz for her physical therapy.

"Her recovery will take time." He hauled his own load of sand out toward the field. They'd picked up five bags, which was probably too many, but it didn't hurt to be prepared.

"No, us. The three of us. She doesn't think it will work." Logan's barely-there limp seemed more pronounced. They'd grab the wheelbarrow on the way out for the next load.

"What did you do?" He dropped his bag next to the mound and stared at his best friend. The man pushed too hard. He'd forced his way through his own recovery, fighting every step of the way, and seemed determined to do the same thing to Jazz.

"I didn't do anything. She's been pulling away from us. I told her I wasn't going to let her do that. She thinks her scars make her ugly. She's worried about how the TBI is affecting her physically. I wanted her to know that she's gorgeous and that hell yes, I still want her." The note of defensive worry echoed in the way Logan slung the bag onto the ground.

"Yeah, but the two of you were together last night...."

"Because I urged it. I didn't really give her a chance to say no. But something is off—she's fighting harder to get on her feet. Which is good." Logan didn't pace. He went the completely opposite route to almost total motionlessness.

Shoving the baseball cap out of his eyes, Zach studied his friend. "But?"

"But what if she's pushing because she wants to get away from us?"

The thought never occurred to him. It sounded insane. Why would Jazz want to get away? Get back to work, that made sense. "Did she say that?"

"Not in as many words, no. But she did say it wasn't going to work—that if she was with me, she had to be with you—I didn't really let her finish it. Fuck. I shouldn't have pushed." For Logan to be questioning himself worried Zach almost as much as what it was that Jazz said or didn't.

Sliding the knife from his back pocket, he flicked out a blade and cut open one of the sandbags. "Let me ask you this. How did you think it was going to work with the three of us?" He didn't know his own answer to that question. It occurred to him that he'd made a lot of assumptions. The future wasn't something either planned for when they'd been in the service.

"The way it did in Vegas. The three of us together." The answer came swiftly. And so did the suspicion. "Did you have other plans?"

"Not particularly. She's—everything. But we haven't spent more than a few hours with her together until now. We had those weekends, but it was like you had yours and then I had mine. Talking to her, getting her emails—we shared those." He cut into the second bag before clicking the knife closed.

Logan grabbed the bag Zach opened and began spreading the sand. The morning sun shone down on the hazy, humid morning. If it kept up with the rain, he was going to have to put in a request for a tarp to cover the field. "Right. Does it bother you that she was in my bed last night?"

"No." But that wasn't completely honest. The twinge in his gut warned him of the lie and he sighed. "Okay, maybe a little. But more because I wanted to join—and didn't think I should push it."

"You were welcome, you know that, right?" Logan stared at him.

"By you, sure. But would she have wanted it?" It seemed neither of them had an answer to that one. "Look, if she only wants one of us, I don't have a problem with that." Yeah, that was more than a little lie. He wasn't sure he knew how to untangle his emotions from the woman he was in love with.

"I'm not sure." His best friend shook his head grimly. "We can make this work. We just have to convince her we can—if you're still in?"

It annoyed the hell out of Zach to answer that question. "Is there some reason you keep thinking I'm going to bail on this situation?"

"No, but I think if she's not convinced the three of us can work. We have to prove it to her. The only way we do that is coordinated effort." Logan nodded slowly as they traded out the empty sand bags for rakes. "In fact, I think we need a plan of attack."

"Surgical or blitz?" Zach grinned.

"Blitz. She's so focused on her recovery, we're going to need shock and awe to overwhelm her. She needs us. I don't know why she thinks she has to choose, but we drive her to the only choice that matters and that's both of us. Son of a bitch! What do you say we take our lady on a date?"

Zach laughed. He really hoped Jazz wasn't too married to the idea of choosing. "What did you have in mind?"

☘

"Maybe you need a pros and cons list." Stormer's phone call was the lifeline Jasmine hadn't realized she needed. "You know, what's great about them, what's not great. What do they bring to the bedroom individually?"

"The sex is awesome and not open for discussion." But she laughed at the Marine's blasé tone. "And they're both so different, but they support me. They drive me. They take care of me. They care about what I think...they've never treated me as less than a Marine."

"Fuck, honey, if you don't want both, give me one. I could use a guy right about now. I'm stuck here filing paper and training the new girl. She cannot get over the idea that we're not supposed to sell pop rocks and American burgers to these people."

"When's Roxy due back?" She missed them. She'd met both Marines before the FET assignment, but six months of working in close quarters together developed into the first real female friendships she'd enjoyed in the Corps. Roxy clucked like a mother hen, and Stormer approached everything with the same droll, dry humor. But they'd clicked.

"One more week. Her little girl had appendicitis, so she got some hardship time to stick around through the recovery."

A lifer, Roxy was one of the lucky ones. Her husband didn't mind playing stay-at-home dad to their three kids while running some mini-internet empire. She could have opted out at any time after her third child was born, but the woman was a Marine through and through. She loved her kids, but she also loved the Corps.

"Yeah, well you may be stuck with new girl for a while, so break her in gently." Jazz transferred the phone to her left ear and worked, squeezing the ball with her right hand. It satisfied the urge to do something while helping the strength in her fingers to return.

"Honey, if I had two guys willing to lick me from my toenails to my boobs and everywhere in between, I'd make me break in the new girl, too."

God, she loved Stormer. The woman approached every issue in pure black and white. "You're still not getting details about the sex. But yeah—" She attributed the heat on her cheeks to the sun overhead. Her physical therapy had ended twenty minutes before, and she kicked back in her wheelchair outside the center. She'd sent a text to Logan that she was done, and he promised he was on his way. It seemed weird that he wasn't right there when she finished as he had been every other time. "They're probably the only really awesome part of this crap."

"Bed rest in air conditioning with real coffee and hot guys—gotta say I'm not really feeling your pain."

Jazz laughed. She pictured Stormer's eyes crossing as she delivered that line. "Mocking the wounded is not an honorable pastime."

"True. But neither is telling me you have problems choosing which guy to fuck."

Point taken.

"Miss you."

"Yeah, me, too. Oh, look. New girl is back and she forgot her helmet...again." The long suffering sigh carried a wicked sense of humor. "And there she goes back to her locker. Point goes to her, she got the message without having to be told."

"Don't get dead, Mary." She was reluctant to hang up, but those few minutes brightened the pall on her self-pity.

"Right back atcha."

The phone clicked as she hung up, and Jazz stared at it. It sucked for her friends to be there, when she couldn't cover their backs. Knowing they hadn't been injured in the attack saved her sanity. Learning that most of the girls they'd talked to that day, including little Anoonseh, signed up for the next batch of classes almost made it worth it. They'd been furious on her behalf—furious and grateful. Anoonseh's mother even sent a private message of thanks, which Stormer relayed to her along with the news that she was going to take classes with her daughter.

She'd made a difference. It wasn't as much as she wanted it to be, but she had done it. She clung to that.

"Jasmine Winters?" A delicate, feminine voice intruded and she glanced up into the single, most cheerful smile she'd ever seen. A stunning blonde in jeans and a loose blousy shirt stood in front of her, sunglasses perched on her head like a headband. "I'm Lauren Kincaid."

"James' Lauren?" She accepted the beautifully manicured hand stretching out to take hers and shook it.

"Yes, I am." The woman's smile increased, if that were possible, and she radiated good cheer and positive health. Dazzled by the wattage, Jazz smiled back. "I've been wanting to meet you ever since the boys brought you up at dinner a few months ago. But James insisted I wait until you had some recovery time. He thinks I bulldoze every situation. Which is true, but sometimes it takes a good bulldozer to plow through the bullshit. You know what I mean?"

"Actually, yes, I do. It's nice to meet you. I think Zach mentioned you in a letter—or maybe it was Logan? They were impressed with James' ability to land a 'movie babe.'" Probably not the most complimentary way of putting it, but Lauren laughed.

"I am the one who totally got lucky. Anyway, not that I can't talk about James all day, but I'm actually here to pick you up."

"Me?" Jazz frowned. Logan might be running late—a first—but she didn't recall making any other plans. A frisson of fear struck sparks against her gut. Was she still losing time?

She didn't think she had in the last couple of weeks.

"Yes, and before you start worrying you forgot something, this is totally spontaneous. I was walking James to his office when we ran into the guys. They were on their way here and mentioned you. I am seriously in need of a manicure and some pampering, so I thought to myself what better way to get to know you than to invite you along?" She waved a clearly-not-in-need-of-a-manicure hand for emphasis. "I have this great place I go to, we can get massages, some mani-pedis, and they'll serve us lunch to boot. Say yes? I don't have a lot of girlfriends here to do this with except for Rebecca, and she's neck deep in wedding planning. I'd rather have a mud facial than be up to my armpits in taffeta."

Everything about the glowing woman from her glossy blonde locks pulled back in a casual ponytail, to her sparkling sandals framing bright red toenails was like being struck blind by a hurricane of cheer. "Okay, I need to call the guys...."

"Nope. No need. I told them I'd take you back to the apartment if you said no, so you're free." She cocked her head, sweeping a completely nonjudgmental look over her appearance. "Unless you want to change. I didn't think about the fact that you worked out. I have some things that might fit then we can play a little dress up while we're at it."

Dazed by the effervescence, Jazz laughed again. "No, I'm good. I actually managed to use one of the showers in the center."

"Perfect! Are you good to go or do I get to push? I warn you, I will make back up beeps if we have to turn around."

The complete impudence in the tease tickled Jazz's funny bone. "I think I got this. Where are you parked?"

Chapter Eight

*J*azz relaxed. The masseuse turned out to be in the Air Force reserve and understood the physical therapy she was undergoing. Ninety minutes of toning massage later, she felt better than she had in weeks. Amber dug her thumbs and elbows into knots along Jazz's spine, triggering pressure points that hurt like a bitch at first, but when they let go, she thought she'd peed.

By the time she poured off the table and they wheeled her out to the mani-pedi room, she felt almost human. Amber wrapped her head in a warm towel, covering the scars and the spiky stubble length of her hair. It was growing back, very, very slowly. Jazz maneuvered onto the pedi chair without any assistance. Amber, bless her, stayed close but somehow managed not to hover.

"I am in love with this spa." Lauren occupied the opposite chair, her hair pulled up into a ponytail at the back of her head. A Marine green headband held the tendrils off her scrubbed face.

"It's pretty nice." It was more than nice. The spa seemed to cater every need a woman might have from hair to body massage.

"I was thinking facials after this, are you doing okay for

that?" Lauren's bright and sunny personality steam rolled over any possible objections, so Jazz just smiled.

"Sure." Of course, it occurred to her that she didn't have her wallet or a way to pay. Straightening in the chair, she glanced down at the petite Asian woman who turned on the water and warm jets.

"Don't worry about it" Lauren interrupted her before she could protest. "Membership has its privileges."

"You're very good at that." Jazz leaned back again and sighed as her feet settled into the warm water.

"Which *that* are we discussing?" Lauren inspected the pink polish on her nails. "Does this look too Pepto to you?"

"No, they look more delicate that that. Pepto kind of screams at you." The bizarre conversation added another layer of surreal to the early afternoon escape. The first was the conspicuous absence of the guys. A hollow ache wrapped around her heart. They hadn't called either. Maybe Logan more than got her message the night before—even though they'd had sex—mind blowing sex. She didn't know who to choose or even how.

But God, she didn't want to lose them. It hurt.

"Good. So what were you saying?" Lauren dragged her back to the presence. The pedicurist slathered warm wax on her legs and she glanced down.

"You seem very confident in your ability to get your way. You make a decision and everyone rushes to comply. Even me, apparently." The last words rode a droll and dry note. "Not that I'm complaining."

"Are you sure? It sounded a bit like a complaint." The blonde squinted and wrinkled her nose, but her smile never faltered.

"I'm positive. It never occurred to me to do this. Amber is an amazing masseuse. I'm feeling pretty good...ow!" She jerked her gaze down to the pedicurist who was not working on Jazz's feet, but waxing her legs. "A little warning next time."

A shiver of déjà vu raced up her spine. She'd done this before. In Las Vegas, the day she met them, she'd spent an entire day in a spa. She'd been plucked, plumped, primped and primed for her night. She'd walked down that long hallway from the elevator to the hotel room in a cloud of femininity. She'd wanted to feel sexy and like a woman. The spa helped.

Zach and Logan did the rest.

"Jazz?" Lauren's voice penetrated the haze of pleasure the memory evoked, and she focused on the present.

"I'm fine. Wasn't expecting that."

"Tell her if it hurts too much. I know you've been stuck in the hospital or at the PT center. I figured the whole female package would enjoy a little pampering." The woman's frankness was absolutely priceless. "But you push back anytime you think we're going across the line."

"I will. To be honest...I think I did need this. It's not the first thing that occurs to me." And it wasn't. Her mother despaired of her as a teen when she preferred the rough sports to more girly activities. She'd barely done more than pony tail her hair for prom, and she spent her eighteenth birthday with the Marine recruiter, signing paperwork. The only thing standing between her and Parris Island had been her high school graduation.

She belonged to the Marines. She found a strength and a purpose with her brothers and sisters- in-arms that she'd found nowhere else.

Except Las Vegas...and you didn't even realize they were Marines.... Her heart twinged. She'd loved being with them, loved it so much that she'd nearly been late to her meeting to re-sign her contract. She loved it so much that she'd actually hesitated to re-sign. *I never told them that. I had lunch with them after, but I never told them I almost didn't do it. They never asked me not too either. They asked me to keep in touch. They wanted to visit on my leaves. They wanted to know where I would be assigned, and they knew what questions to ask. But they never asked me to not be me.*

She barely noticed the waxing as the woman finished, or when she started on her toenails. Her mind whirled with information. The lonely ache in her soul intensified. Every time a door opened, she glanced up, half-expecting to see them. Either. Both. But they didn't come.

Two hours later, she reclined in yet another chair with goop on her face to open her pores and repair the skin. The technician performing the facial clucked over her, equal parts admiration for her skin tone and admonishment for not taking better care of it. Jazz didn't laugh. She'd chosen the same red for her nails she'd worn in Vegas. It wasn't regulation. She should have chosen clear, but the first time she saw that red peeking out of the manicurist basket, she'd wanted it.

It would be better if she planned to put on that sassy black dress, but it was packed away at her mom's. She could call her, but what would she say. *Hey mom, I know I'm still learning this walking thing, but I want to dress up and get laid. You know like that Vegas trip you bought me?*

Yeah, no.

Her mother worried enough about her. She loved her mom. They may not always have understood each other or been on the same page, but her mother never made her feel bad about her choices. Not even when that choice included two men. Pastor Robbie wouldn't feel the same way, nor would most of the members of her mother's church. Hell, if she couldn't reconcile the idea that she loved two men, wanted both, and desired a way to be with the two of them forever, how would anyone else?

But what if it isn't forever? The tiny note of self-doubt crept out of the shadows of her soul. *What if this is a fling? I'm assuming they're looking at forever, too. But two guys don't plan to be with the same woman for the long term, no matter how great they are. Logan said he wasn't jealous of Zach, but what happens when—if I get pregnant? That changes things. Do I want to get pregnant?*

The thought made her feel vaguely ill. Children, like marriage, were concepts she'd put off to a nebulous future. When she completed her military service, or at least until the action in Afghanistan and Iraq abated. Not that there seemed to be a long-term end coming anytime soon.

"You realize the point of this, the dark room, the mood music, the treatments—it's to wind down. Not wind up, right?" Lauren chided her in a hushed voice. "I can hear you thinking from here."

They were alone in the facial room, their treatments working while wind chimes and ocean waves accompanied a soft piano concerto. Jazz barely noticed the music until Lauren brought it up. "I think this is the first time I've felt alone enough in my head to think things through."

"Hmm, too much background noise. Recovery. Doctors. Nurses. Physical therapists. Hot guys. I imagine that's pretty overwhelming. I feel that way a lot when I'm on set. I have to pack Lauren away and immerse myself in the character or I'll go crazy. It's worse at big events or when there's a huge press presence. You can't frown thinking about something, whether it's the picture or if you've paid your electrical bill, because someone snaps a shot and begins to speculate—usually wildly speculate." No self-pity presented itself in her words, just simple acceptance of her life. "James isn't particularly fond of the press part, but he's amazing when we have to do it. He gives them this stern, firm look and they back up obediently. Marines are so sexy."

Jazz teetered on the edge of laughter, but her chuckle echoed with unshed tears, and she blinked rapidly to force them back. "The guys are great. They have been more than great. They stuck around even when I gibbered like a gibbon. They take care of me. They bathe me. They feed me. They drive me to all my appointments. They're great."

Pushy Lauren returned. "But?"

"It's not worth complaining about." They weren't screwing anything up. She was.

"Of course it is. I don't care how much someone loves you. If they hover, it can get annoying. Those guys are good looking men, you don't want to look like a patient to them or someone they have to take care of, you want to be sexy and attractive." Score another point to the bubbly blonde. Her cheerful attitude disguised a very sharp and observant mind.

Jazz's mouth tightened. "It's not that simple." *Logan definitely made me feel attractive last night.* Her body warmed at the memory, the feeling of his hands caressing her, teasing her nipples, stroking her sides, and the hard intensity in his eyes when he slid his cock inside her. She shifted against the chair, a little mortified at the tension coiling through her. She wanted him right now. She wanted to feel him thrusting inside of her while she kissed Zach.

Damn it. She ordered her body to stand down, but her brain continued its decadent assault of images.

"It may not be simple. I'm not a Marine. I don't know what it takes to go through what you've been through. But I can try to draw parallels to understand better, and I'm really good at listening."

Jazz turned her head to the right and looked at her roommate. Her hair was hidden beneath a towel and her face was the color of lime with speckles of dirt sprinkled on top. She didn't look remotely glamorous, yet she still appeared utterly feminine. "It's not about being a Marine. It's not even about the IED. It's about them and me loving both of them. It's about not being able to choose between them and wondering if I'm making more out of this than there is."

"How so?" Lauren sat up, ignoring the whole kick back and relax atmosphere and sat sideways in the chair.

"What if it's a fling? What if I should stop worrying about who to pick and just enjoy it while it lasts?" She hated how self-involved that sounded, but they'd never talked about what came next. They chatted about Mike's Place, the theatre, her assignment, Zach's sport teams, Logan's plans to finish his certification as a physical therapist. They talked about their individual goals and accomplishments. They never talked about the three of them.

"Would it bother you if it was only a fling?" Uncaring of her face mask, Lauren propped her chin into her hand while her elbow rested on one raised knee.

"I...." She thought hard about the answer to that. The sinking feeling in her gut screamed that yes that was a problem. But if she didn't see herself with two men long-term, why wouldn't it be an issue for then as well? "Realistically...."

"No. Not realistically. In your heart, does it bother you? Your face fell when I asked that question. So would it bother you?"

Jazz wanted to look away from her, but the woman had presence. She demanded attention. It probably explained her success as an actress, not that she'd seen any of her films. But more than that, she wanted to answer the question. "Yeah. It would bother me. As selfish as it sounds, I don't want to be only a fling. They're—they're amazing, sexy, sweet, honorable men. They make me laugh. They make me want to be more. They make me want more."

"So what's the problem?" The words echoed James' question from every single session so clearly that she could almost hear his more masculine tone overlaying Lauren's sweeter voice.

"Realism. A long-term relationship requires equal time, equal respect, and equality. It's hard to be equal when there's three...and who gets married? Who gets to be dad? If I get pregnant and it's Zach's—won't Logan feel left out? What if it's Logan's? Legally, I can't marry two men and hell, I don't even know if I want to get married or have kids."

She hated this weak, wishy-washy shit. She needed to make a fucking decision and live with it. But every time she thought about making a choice, her stomachache came back and her head began to pound. She'd break out into a cold sweat. She didn't want to lose either man. She didn't want to come between them.

"I can't say I understand, because for me it's James. I don't want any other guy. Ever. I've seen open relationships that worked. Hollywood is full of them. I know this one couple who are amazing parents, amazingly in love and he has lovers—male lovers—but lovers. She doesn't mind. Because they committed to something between them and they're happy. I know other couples that lie all day long about how happy they are and go home to ignore each other. We paint a picture of what a romance is supposed to look like, and then we put them under a microscope and judge them if they don't conform to that picture. But life isn't a painting. It's messy and dirty and filled with warts. No one can tell you that a long-term relationship with those guys isn't a possibility except them and you. Have you talked to them about it?"

Jazz stared at her. If the actress sprouted two heads and four arms, she wouldn't have been remotely surprised. "It doesn't bother you that I'm even considering it?"

"Honey, I'm not the one who has to sleep with them, and what you do in the privacy of your home can't possibly affect what I do in the privacy of mine. So why should it? If they want you and you want them—then go for it."

A light knock announced their specialist returning, and Jazz twisted to point at the woman. "We need a few more minutes."

"Um...the masks need to come off."

Lauren joined her in sending the woman away. "Our pores can use a little more tightening. Shoo." The technician shook her head, but retreated, and closed the door behind her. "Jasmine, have you talked to them?"

"No. I tried to—no—I didn't try hard enough. Because I'm not sure I want the answer." The confession cost her. She didn't know Lauren well enough to share those kinds of details, but the woman inspired a trust she hadn't experienced outside of her fellow Marines.

"Then talk to them. Don't mince your words. Lay your cards on the table. You're killing yourself because you want something you think you can't—or shouldn't—have. That's a pointless exercise."

"And if I don't like the answer, well that sucks balls, but at least I'll have it." *Boots up, Marine.*

"You know, there's the very real possibility that it can work. Those two are close, closer than brothers. They do everything together. They respect each other. They support each other. James told me that without Zach, Logan wouldn't have survived what he went through. From what I've seen, if Logan hadn't survived—neither would Zach. So remember that. Now. This mask is itching."

"Yeah.... Lauren?"

"Hmm?"

"Thank you." She didn't have to try and inject gratitude or sentiment into those two words.

"You're very welcome. Would it be rude to ask for details at some point? You know, purely for research?"

Jazz laughed and the bruising ache in her soul eased. She would talk to them.

She would talk to them both tonight.

သ

"Everything ready?" Logan stood in the doorway fumbling with his tie while Zach polished his shoes.

"Damon gave us the green light. He's got the private room set up. We'll be serving ourselves so we don't have any interruptions, and I have the keys to his apartment if we decide to scoot out his secret back door."

Logan nodded slowly. "James called. Lauren will drop her off at the restaurant in a couple of hours. They had to stop for shoes. He promised me that she swore she wasn't shopping for herself."

They'd debated setting up a hotel room, like their night in Vegas, but as much as they wanted to recapture that night— they wanted to set the stage for something bigger. Damon's restaurant, Lagniappe's, offered the best compromise. Private dining area, romantic setting, secret escape route, and a fully stocked bedroom for ménage shenanigans should they choose to indulge.

Zach planned a great deal of indulgence. They also had the restaurant to themselves. So if they got frisky in the private area, no one would be listening or looking. He was surprised the chef offered to shut the place down for them, but like the rest of their Marines, everyone was on board with helping Jazz—and them.

Good men. Every single one of them.

"You have your ring?" Zach checked his pocket for the service ring he'd stowed away in there.

Logan tapped his chest. "It's with the dog tags. I got yours and attached one on there, too."

"Good." The plan would take some coordination. Good food, beer, although water for her since her meds didn't allow for alcohol yet, music, dancing, and enough sex to put her fears to rest.

"She could say no." Trust his best friend to bring up the only real downside to the plan. If she really wanted out of this relationship, all she had to do was shut them down.

"She won't." He said it with a hell of a lot more confidence than he felt. "We're not going to let her."

"Power of positive thinking?" Tie secure, Logan walked over to borrow a brush and added a little polish to his own wingtips. They hated the suits, but they were perfect for the romantic atmosphere the two spent the day arranging. Dress blues would be better, but they were making a civilian proposal. So, civilian uniforms it was.

"Power of positive planning. She has objections. We take care of them. She has fears. We comfort them. She has needs. We meet them. She belongs to us. We have to remind her of that fact."

"The next time I give you shit about being little Miss Mary Sunshine, remind me of this moment." Logan held out his hand. "May the best men win."

"We are the few and the proud. That definitely makes us the best." Zach shook his hand. "And don't worry, I will definitely remind your sourpuss about all the times I've been right."

Chapter Nine

*I*nstead of taking her back to Mike's Place, Lauren pulled up in front of a restaurant called Lagniappes. A sign announcing 'Closed for Business' filled the upper half of the glass door. "I don't think your stardom is going to be enough to get us through a line that doesn't exist."

The ninety-minute shoe odyssey to find a pair of black, peep-toe flats to show off her pedicure, and the insistence on a dress seemed based on an ulterior motive. So did the colorful scarf Lauren produced to replace her baseball cap. She enjoyed the woman's direct-indirectness, however, so she didn't argue. It was time to go home and she wanted to see the guys. Resolute to confront this issue head on, it made more sense to strike while the iron was hot.

"Alas, you are correct." Lauren ruined her dramatic sigh and pause for effect by giggling. "It's your stardom that matters here. Ah, here come your escorts now."

The air whooshed out of her lungs as Zach and Logan stepped out of the restaurant. They were dressed identically in button down suits, ties, and slacks right down to the color. The dress blue shade matched their ties and created a stark contrast to the white shirts beneath.

"Have a great time tonight. I don't expect to hear from you

before the weekend, but I want all the details." Lauren's bubbling enthusiasm must be contagious, because excitement churned in Jazz's stomach.

"Thanks for today." She spared the woman a last glance before Zach caught the door and pulled it wide. Logan extended a hand, and she let him help her out. "Oh, I should get the wheelchair."

"No need, I can drop it off!" Lauren waved and pulled away as soon as Zach closed the door.

The warm evening air ruffled her neck. The scarf tickled her skin, but the sensation didn't match the sight of these two men, so different in coloring and stance, yet so very alike standing in front of her.

"Hey."

Zach hadn't expected the donkey kick to his midsection when he opened the door. Logan's relaxed air didn't seem to invade his own rattled nerves or pounding heart. But as Logan took her hand and helped her to stand, the uncertainty washed away in a torrent of lust, affection, and respect. The fear churning in his gut since Brody's phone call, exacerbated by the sight of her fragile, pale features as her Navy escort wheeled her down the concourse, settled.

The long road to full recovery still stretched out in front of them, but light sparkled in her brown eyes. A smile flirted with her lips. Her red dress with its forties square top, tied behind her neck, cupped her breasts beautifully and emphasized the slender column of her neck. She'd lost some muscle tone, but it left her with softer, almost lusher curves.

He didn't know squat about fashion, but she looked good. Red was definitely her color. Logan leaned down and slanted his mouth across hers for a kiss. The seconds ticked by and her hand bunched around his lapel. The soft sigh she released as he stepped back, went straight to Zach's cock.

"My turn." He grinned and Logan edged aside as Zach carefully cupped her face in his hands and teased her with a light kiss. If he went any deeper with full public display lewdness, he was in real danger of blowing their plan. Her lips parted beneath his, but he didn't press the advantage, enjoying the taste of mint and lemon that lingered on her breath. Heat flushed his skin, and she seemed brighter when he lifted his head. "Hey."

"Wow." Her laughter stoked his passion even as it relaxed the steel bands compressing his chest. "Hi."

"We're glad you could join us." Logan tucked her hand on the crook of his arm, and Zach mirrored the gesture. They walked her to the door, measuring their steps as if they'd practiced to match her uneven gait. Logan let her go long enough to open the door, and Zach guided her through. Logan turned the lock behind them and adjusted the door's curtains to shield them from prying eyes. Inside the shadowy restaurant, they strolled up a pathway to the private dining area illuminated by candles on either side.

The chef had outdone himself. The private dining room boasted a round table, plush chairs, and enough food to make Zach's mouth water. When Jazz's stomach growled audibly, he didn't bother to disguise his laughter.

"You like?" he asked edging around them to pull out a chair. She'd done great on her walk. Strength and confidence returning with every step, but they didn't want to overdo it. No, they had plans for this evening, and they did not include exhausting her.

Not yet, anyway.

"It's—wow—that's a lot of food." In addition to the steaks, there was lobster tail, gumbo, shrimp, heaping platters of steamed vegetables, red-roasted potatoes, and warm bread. Her stomach rumbled again, and she flattened her hand against it. "Excuse me."

"No excuses needed. Would you allow us the honor of serving you this evening?" The increase in her appetite was a great sign. Zach watched Logan in those first few weeks after his surgeries. When he started getting hungry again, it meant he'd turned a corner. He only hoped the same spoke true for Jazz.

Her gaze flicked back and forth between them. "I'd love it."

Zach released a breath he hadn't realized he'd been holding. Logan steadied her chair, and she sat, slowly and gracefully. Her skirt scooted up over her legs and bared a portion of her thigh. In an effort not to swallow his tongue, he forced his attention to ride back up to her face. The little minx grinned at him.

Hot damn, was their Jazz back after a day at a spa? If he'd suspected that effect, they would have made arrangements for it a whole lot sooner.

"Did you have a good day?" Logan elbowed him into moving again and followed so they loaded up the plates.

"It was interesting. I would never have imagined Lauren and James. He's so quiet and she's so...enthusiastic. But she's fun, too. I'm guessing none of the beer is for me, huh?" The question tweaked Zach's guilt, but her dry humor eased the sting.

"Not yet." Logan pointed to the veggies. Jazz liked her veggies, but Zach waved him off and added the lobster tail to the steak. The woman preferred her meat.

"Boring." Her amusement turned them both around, but she held a glass of water and drank it. "I can't do the bottle trick if I'm stuck with water."

Zach laughed. "You don't need tricks." They carried the plates back and set them up, taking their seats on either side of her. The romantic setting was unsettling. He preferred the diner or their own kitchen table. But Lagniappes served a purpose, too.

"Oh, sweet. I'll be big as a barn when I'm done." Not that it slowed her down from claiming her fork and knife. She cut into the steak, and Zach watched the knife in her right hand, cautious. It trembled. He flexed his fingers around the chilled beer bottle and ignored Logan's kick under the table. They weren't supposed to hover.

But he also didn't want her hand to spasm, slip, and cut her.

When she lifted a piece to her mouth, he relaxed his vigilant watch and met Logan's narrowed gaze. Her groan went straight to his cock, and he shifted his weight in the seat to ease the pressure on his balls.

"This is excellent. How did you get the owner to let us eat on a night when they're closed?"

"We know people." Logan grinned. Zach admired how easily Logan fell into this role. His relaxed posture and easy expressions belied the man who scowled and worried that she would say 'no' earlier.

"Yeah? You going to introduce me?" Jazz took a sip of water before transferring her attention to the lobster tail.

"Eventually. Damon's out with his lady tonight, so he gave us run of the restaurant. I'm pretty sure he fixed most of the food, though." He forced an exhale between his teeth and set to work on cutting his own meat. Across the table, Logan did the same. "We mentioned we wanted to do something special and take you out on a date, so he did us a solid."

Her fork paused midway to her mouth. The hesitation lasted only a couple of seconds, but he noticed it all the same. "Okay, I'll bite. Date?"

"You know, two or more getting together for a social event to explore the possibility of romance? Emphasis on the exploration aspect."

Zach nearly choked on his beer at Logan's amused delivery.

"I see, so your plan is to wine me, dine me, and sixty-nine me?" The challenge in her voice didn't escape either of them. Logan sat forward and Zach's cock stiffened enthusiastically. He could handle all of the above.

"Something like that."

Way to vague that up, Logan.

"Interesting." But she didn't look at them, her concentration on her food as she cut another piece of steak.

Worry nibbled along the back of Zach's mind. Maybe Logan was right. Maybe she did want out.

"Not really. We'd do this for you every night, but you haven't been ready." Time to cut through the crap. "Or at least we didn't think you were."

"So why tonight? What made you decide that I was *up* for it tonight?" Jazz examined another bite. Her mild tone rang a warning bell in Zach's mind. He glanced at Logan, but his friend stared at Jazz and didn't see the question on his face.

"Because you seem to have the idiotic impression that this can't work, and we're not in a relationship for the long haul."

Zach winced. *Yeah, that's gonna come back to bite us.*

The setting, the food, even the way they were dressed, left her tingling in anticipation. It was hard to mistake the naked heat in Zach's expression for anything but lust and affection. Logan's casual touches, a brush of his thumb across her bare arm, and the stroke of his fingers at the nape of her neck as she sat down, intensified the emotions surging in her belly. Even the food tasted of seduction. She fully intended to broach the topic of their relationship, what she desired out of it, what she hoped, and how they could make it work. But the luxurious setting, the meal, and their formal dress threw her an unexpected curve ball.

She couldn't bring herself to spoil their efforts. At least until Logan went on the offensive. Setting her fork and knife down, she dabbed at her mouth—careful to not remove the lipstick—and focused on the intensity blazing in Logan's eyes.

"I'm sorry. My 'what' impression?" He deserved the opportunity to revise that statement.

"What Logan meant to say is, we're concerned about where you believe this relationship between us is headed. We would like to have a chance to discuss it, over dinner." Zach's attempt at peacemaker might have worked, but Logan snorted.

"No, that isn't what Logan meant to say." His use of the third person in reference to himself might have been funny, except that his tone was anything but. "You questioned our honor and our integrity."

"I did not." Her own temper kindled under the heat sparking in Logan's. "I said I didn't know how this could work or how I could choose between you."

"You don't have to choose, Jazz. Ease up, Logan." Zach's peacemaking barely put a dent in the smoke rising from the impending conflagration.

"That's easy to say right now. I get it. You both help me and you've both been amazing. But how the hell do we make this work long term? I'm still fighting a wheelchair and my brain. You two think we can just set up house until...what? You each meet a woman who only wants you? Then what happens?" Fear sank its teeth into her spine. "I fucked Logan last night, so by those terms, I should fuck Zach tonight. But taking turns only delays the inevitable."

Had she really thought they would be a threesome? It was hardly legal, definitely not moral, and the ethics involved were so skewed, they gave her a headache.

"You don't have to choose, woman." Logan's hand cracked down on the table and made the glasses jump. "We've all but told you that. We're a package deal. It's both of us or neither of us."

Her spine stiffened at the threat in his words. Logan painted a very black and white picture. But they didn't live in a black and white world.

"Then maybe I should move out of the apartment until we sort this out." Her voice was eerie calm. Calmer than she was, at least, and betrayed none of the turmoil knotting in her belly. Her appetite vanished in the heat of the battle, and what little food she'd consumed sat in her stomach like a rock.

"Enough." Zach's voice cracked like a whip through the tension. Jazz jerked her gaze to him, and his glare seemed to encompass both her and Logan. "This was not supposed to be a fight or an accusation. It's about resolving the issues between us, putting our cards and on the table, and deciding on a plan to get what we want—what all *three* of us want."

Jazz refused to fidget, but the muscle ticking in Zach's jaw betrayed his tension. Logan's noisy exhale dragged her attention to him. His tight expression revealed the struggle to hold onto his temper.

"Now, Jazz. Truth or dare?"

She twisted in her seat and met the challenge rising in Zach's blue eyes. They gleamed with focus, and if she were less a Marine, she might even have squirmed under the harsh attention.

"What?" She regulated her breathing and flexed her hands against the napkin. She wasn't sure she could eat more at the moment, not with the agitation churning in her gut.

"Truth or dare?" Zach repeated, the corner of his mouth slipping up into a smile. "It's a game. I'm sure you recall the rules."

"Dare." If he wanted to play a game, fine. She'd play.

"I dare you to kiss Logan and make up." His lashes lowered in challenge.

"All right." She shoved her chair back and tossed her napkin down. With a hell of a lot more control than she felt, she stood and looked down at Logan. He pushed his own chair back, staring at her. Defiance stiffened her spine and she met his glare. He wanted a kiss, by God, she'd give him a kiss.

Her right foot dragged, hitching her step, and she braced herself with a hand on his shoulder. He clamped a grip down on her hip and a thrill shivered over her nerves as she leaned down and brushed her lips against his. She intended for it to be a soft, quick peck. But his grip shifted and skated up her spine, and she all but fell into his lap. His mouth opened, and his tongue invaded her mouth.

A rush of heat stabbed at her senses, and he took possession of the kiss, demanding her response. He caught the back of her head in a gentle but immovable hold. His tongue stroked hers, twined around it. The kiss tasted of anger—but also of need and desire. He demanded her attention, her acquiescence, and her affection.

Just as quickly as the blaze consumed her, so did the gentle way he held her, steady and solid. She would never fall while he had his arms around her. His temper gave way to teasing and when he sucked on her tongue, pulling it against his teeth, pleasure rippled from her breasts to her sex. When he pulled his head back, his eyes were dark with want.

"Your turn." The husky timbre skated across her skin like a caress. She glanced over at Zach. He watched them both with a satisfied expression, but his blue eyes were blazing hot.

She tried to clear her throat, but a lump of emotion and desire seemed to be clogging her voice. "Truth or dare?"

"To which one of us, sweetheart?" Zach licked the lobster bite from his fingers, and she stared at his tongue action. Her thighs trembled. God, they really did turn her upside down with almost no effort.

"You." She managed to force the word out. Logan's hand cupped her ass as he settled her on his lap. She should climb out of it, but she wasn't sure her legs would hold her after that.

"Hmm." Zach took a swallow of beer. "Truth."

Her mind blanked. "Um...how did my kissing Logan make you feel?"

His slow grin seemed answer enough, but he leaned forward and pinned her against Logan with his gaze. "Hot. Turned on. Stiff as a board. Watching you kiss him is sexy as hell."

The words and the look set a wave of wet heat through her. She longed to kiss him. To stoke the flames burning in her belly until they all caught fire. She loved them both. She wanted to touch and be touched, to kiss and be kissed, and be naked and to strip them down. The night before with Logan was just the beginning. She needed to touch him—them— more.

"Logan, truth or dare." Zach cut another piece of steak and reached over to tease her lips with it. She opened her mouth and took the bite, never looking away from him as she chewed.

Behind her, Logan laughed. "Truth."

"How do you feel about the orgasms I gave her a few weeks ago?" The dry delivery accompanied by the wryness in his smile sent a squirm of need through her. He had given her orgasms in that shower. Several of them. The light touch of his fingers, the rasp of the washcloth and her body went to putty. Beneath her, Logan's cock stiffened against her bottom.

"Hmm...a little desperate to finish what you started." Logan's breath tickled her cheek and she cut her gaze back to him. "Truth or dare, cupcake?"

"Cupcake?"

"Hmm-hmm. Sweet and glossy frosting that I want to lick off."

Holy shit, desire rode through her, and now she definitely wanted to be naked. She boiled from the inside out.

She should say truth. They needed this conversation. Truth. She would say truth. "Dare."

"Give me your panties and go sit in Zach's lap." The words conjured Vegas. The way he'd knelt down in front of her and stripped her panties off with his teeth. The warmth of his breath and the caress of his lips. The rasp of his stubble against the inside of her thigh. The soft kiss of his mouth to her clit.

Her stomach tightened. She'd have to stay in Logan's lap to get the panties off, standing wasn't really an option. "Can I have help for my dare?"

Logan's arms tightened around her, and he shifted her until she sat with her back to his chest and his erection lay against the seam of her ass. Her stomach plummeted with need, and she fought to concentrate. Logan's fingers splayed against her thighs and rolled her skirt up.

Zach rose from his chair and circled the table. He hooked his fingers into her panties and peeled them down. She had to lift her hips and ground softly against Logan's erection in the process. Chill air teased her heated pussy. She wasn't the only one affected, though. The Marine holding her groaned, and

Zach let loose with a low whistle.

"Someone's wet." He rolled her panties up and stuck them in his pocket. She didn't think she was going to need them anytime soon. He held out a hand to her. Standing took a hell of a lot more effort. He claimed her chair and pulled her into his lap. His fingers caressed up the inside of her thigh until they rested against her sex. The pressure was a torment, because he neither stroked nor pressed his advantage.

"It's your turn to choose, sweetheart." Zach's breath tickled her ear, and she caught Logan's look as he stared at Zach's hand.

"Truth or dare, Logan." Her nipples tightened in anticipation.

"Truth." His hungry stare threatened to gobble her up.

The hell with choices. She wanted them both. "What do you want Zach to do now that I'm in his lap?"

Logan grinned slowly. "Well, he could strip the rest of your clothes off and take his time with your breasts. Tease your nipples until those hard little peaks are flushed pink and ready to be sucked. Or maybe move his hand a little, press down on your clit while he strokes your pussy. Hmm...or better, spread your thighs so I can stare at you and watch while he thrusts his fingers inside and starts stretching you, gets you really wet and slick and ready for his cock."

The words were a slow, torturous sensation. Her body was on fire. Too many damn clothes stood between her and what he described. Zach's fingers flexed against her pussy, a half-frustrating stroke mirroring Logan's suggestion.

"Cruel." Zach's breath seemed to be as shallow as hers was. "Very cruel."

Logan chuckled and scooped a spoonful of lobster out of the shell. He held it to her lips and she opened her mouth to take it. Surprise jerked through her as his mouth slanted over hers and his tongue pursued the juicy shellfish into her mouth. She groaned, straining into the kiss and grinding against Zach. He circled her clit with his thumb, never quite touching it.

Logan pulled away with a chuckle. "Hungry? Maybe we should eat."

"Fuck the food. We're still playing." Her grumble set them both off, and Zach slid a finger down, circling her slick entrance. If their plan was to make her insane, they were on the right road.

"Yeah, fuck the food, Logan. It's your turn." Zach's teeth grazed her earlobe and added another layer to the slow assault on her senses.

"Truth or dare, Jazz."

Oh God, she wanted to say dare. Zach lips massaged her ear. His tongue tracing the whorls drove away coherent thought. "Truth."

"Do you love us?"

The sound of their breathing punctuated the silence stretching between them. Zach went still against her, his thumb grazing her clit. The wonderful caress maddened her. Her pulse pounded. Logan's liquid brown eyes promised pure wickedness but demanded more.

"Jazz?" His lips framed her name and she stared at him. For the first time she really wished she faced both of them at the same time. "Do you love us?"

"Yes."

Chapter Ten

*L*ogan fought the urge to surge forward and kiss her. The declaration was enough. He wanted to bury his cock inside her so deep she forgot what it was like not to have them as a part of her. Tears dampened her cheeks, and worry shifted beneath the laughter sparkling in her eyes. "You love us. So why are you pushing us away?"

"That's two truths." She licked her lips, catching one of the tears creasing along the side of her mouth.

"I don't care about the game. I care about you—we care about you."

"But it's still my turn." Her chin lifted, stubborn pride bringing it up, and Zach's hands glided out to hold her thighs open. Logan didn't want to resist the pretty pink pussy gleaming at him, but he clenched his fist and stayed cemented to his chair.

"Fine. Your turn." He ignored Zach's mouthed 'patience' as he glared at her. If she loved them, there wasn't a problem.

Or there shouldn't be a problem. I don't think we can make it clearer.... Or maybe they could. But a mild resentment he didn't want to own crawled up from his gut to sit on his heart. They would turn themselves inside out for her. If sitting by her bedside day in and day out, helping her with every little thing, not once asking for anything in return wasn't enough—he didn't know how else to prove it. He'd kissed every inch of her body, had stroked her through orgasm after orgasm. He couldn't get enough of her.

He would never have enough of her.

His temper frayed, but he forced the strands back together. She needed him at the top of his game and they had a plan. He would stick to it.

"Okay, truth or dare," she shifted a little, turning her flushed face to look at the man holding her. "Zach."

"Truth."

Patient son of a bitch. Logan blew out a breath through his teeth. His jaws hurt from holding them together, but it was the only way to keep from spitting out every thought in his head.

She glanced back at him once, including him in her question—or at least he hoped that's what it meant. "Where do we go from here? I love you both. I want to be with both of you. But how—how do we make that work?"

Logistics. She was hung up on logistics. Logan pinched the bridge of his nose until his eyes burned. *Of course she's hung up on logistics. She's a gunny. She knows how to look ahead, to look at the angles, to make the plans...c'mon Zach...make the answer count.*

Zach slid a leg back and lifted her, one-arming her onto his leg so she wasn't quite straddling his lap. Logan understood why, but he missed the front row seat to her soft, pink flesh. He adjusted his own seat. The dress trousers weren't designed for a raging hard on. If they convinced her to stay with them, he was going to have to take that into consideration in the next pair.

"It works because we want it to work. We stay honest with each other. You let us love you and share you. It's like Vegas, baby—only we keep it with us forever." Simple and straightforward, Zach didn't pull the verbal punch. "You love us. We love you. We make it work."

Jazz froze, her expression torn between wonder and

disbelief. "You love me?"

Logan's jaw went slack. *I'll be damned. Nailed it.* They'd exposed another vulnerability.

"It's not your turn." Zach smiled at her almost apologetically. "You still wanted to play the game, so if you want that truth or you don't believe what I said, then you can ask again when you get that opportunity."

"Truth or dare, Logan?" Zach interrupted the emotion roiling in his brain.

"Truth." He never looked away from Jazz.

"Do you want to marry her?"

"Hell. Yes." Not even a moment's hesitation creased his thoughts. "Truth or dare, Zach?"

Her attention split as her head turned back and forth between them. Zach stared steadily at her, too.

"Truth." His best friend grinned.

"Do you want to marry her?" Logan knew the answer, but she needed to hear it.

"Abso-freaking-lutely."

"How does that work? I can't marry both of you." Frustration slurred her words.

"Not your turn, darling." Zach kissed the corner of her mouth, and she turned toward him without missing a beat. Her arms wound around his neck, and Logan's temperature climbed with her skirt. Her bottom flashed at him, all smooth pale skin and rounded curves. Although she'd gained back some of the weight she'd lost in the hospital, he wouldn't mind adding a few more pounds to her athletic form.

His palms itched to touch her, and he locked his legs to stay put. *Stick to the plan, Marine.*

Zach pulled back first, his lips mere inches from hers as he stared at her. "Truth or dare Logan?"

"Truth." He practically growled the word.

"Does it matter to you which of us she legally marries?"

"Nope. Jasmine Cavanaugh. Jasmine Evans. They both sound good." He reached across the table and trailed a finger down her bare arm. She turned her sexy face to him, and he grinned at her. "Hell, keep Winters. I don't care what you call yourself as long as you're ours."

"You guys make it sound so damn easy." She shook her head, the blush in her face enhancing the darkness in her eyes.

"No. We're telling you the truth." Logan caught her chin in his hand and urged her to look at him. "Easy is for sissies. We're Marines. We want this to work, we make it work."

"What about kids?"

"What about them?" Zach asked a hell of a lot more gently than Logan would have managed. "Don't think we would make great dads?"

"I think you would make awesome fathers. Both of you. But I can only get pregnant one at a time—what if—what if it matters whose child it is?"

Logan squinted. They'd debated a lot of what went through her head. That subject hadn't come up. He tried to imagine her pregnant, her tummy rounding and swelling with a baby growing in it. His gut jerked at the mental picture. She'd look so fucking gorgeous. It would soften the harder planes of her body, thicken her waist, her hips would spread. His cock strained to the point of pain.

He added the knowledge that it was Zach's baby in her belly. *Would I really care?*

"See, not such an easy question." Jazz bit her lip and her vulnerability struck him.

Her inner strength amazed him. It fueled her struggles, turning her challenges into battles to be overcome—but this mattered to her. *We matter. We matter and if we fuck it up—that's what she's worried about. She doesn't want to hurt us, but she doesn't want to be hurt.*

"We plan." Zach broke the silence, and he held up a hand when she opened her mouth as though to talk. "We plan for it. I'd love your child whether it was mine or his. Hell, fucked up as it sounds, I'd love it if it belonged to some other guy."

Violence flooded Logan at the very idea. He'd strangle any

other man who tried to put his hands on her. But Zach's gaze ordered patience so he kept his mouth shut.

For now.

"We plan for when you get pregnant. We're practically a condom ad now. We don't get pregnant till we decide to do it and then we flip a coin. Or draw straws. Whoever goes first, the other goes second. That means two kids guaranteed, babe. But only if you want them. If you don't want kids, we don't have to have them."

"What if I get pregnant anyway? Condoms break. Accidents happen."

"I am sure as shit not missing out on a life with you based on a 'what if,' Jazz." Logan stood and loomed over both of them. His patience was done. "You're in or you're out. Everything else is crap we can deal with. Marry us. I don't care what the law says or whether we can file it only once, you marry Zach, you're marrying me and vice versa. We're a package deal. What's your answer?"

Zach sighed, but Logan shook his head. They could address her fears all day. Hell, he had more than a few of his own. What did he really know about being a husband? Not crap. But he did know he wanted her—he was never *not* going to want her. They'd let her go after that night in Vegas because one night did not a lifetime make.

But this wasn't a one-night stand. Not anymore.

"You don't have to answer right now." Zach soothed and she appreciated it, more than he knew, but Logan was right. She had to be in this or out of it.

"It would be easier if I trusted my brain." That confession cost, but they deserved to hear it. Logan's glare dimmed and he backed off a step. Pressing a hand to Zach's shoulder for balance, she stood up. Her right leg dragged. It would likely have a bit of a drag from now on, particularly when she was stressed. The doctors warned her that nothing was conclusive. The problem with brain trauma, they knew what it affected, but there were no guarantees in her recovery.

They couldn't predict her progress or her long-term diagnosis. It was one day at a time, one crisis at a time. Her prognosis was far from negative, but it didn't change the position of the rock and hard place sandwiching her.

"See, I don't remember thinking about us as a long-term thing." She smoothed down her skirt. She didn't care about being nude in front of them, but she wanted the barrier, at least while she sorted it out. "I remember living in the moment. Living for the conversations, the talks, the emails— and the leave. But we never talked about forever. We never talked about what it would mean to be all three of us. I want to believe that it will work and that we can make it happen. Like I want to believe that I will gain full function in my arm and my leg. But I don't—life doesn't give us guarantees."

Zach leaned forward, his hands clasped together. This was not how they planned the night. She read it in both their expressions. Logan retreated behind an emotionless mask, his eyes narrowed. Quiet fury radiated off of him.

"You're angry with me for being hurt and for hurting you both. I'm angry at me, too." Up until that moment, she hadn't realized how upset with herself she was. She'd screwed up. She took off her helmet, an IED hit her, and she'd been injured. It could have been so much worse. She could have died or lost a limb.

She looked away from the two of them and limped over to the food. So many mouth watering choices laid out at her fingertips. All she had to do was grab them.

"Jazz?" Of course Zach reached out. Zach who wanted to coddle her, wrap her in cotton, and keep her safe. He never failed to treat her like a lady, even though he respected the fact that she was a Marine. He was quick with the smile, the laugh, and the easy jest.

Logan was harder, edgier, and less forgiving. He demanded so much from himself, it seemed a small wonder that he allowed anyone close to him. He lived with his scars, displayed them proudly, and he didn't let them inhibit him. Battle-forged like steel. Heated until he withstood anything, and he shared that strength as easily as breathing.

"I love you both so much it hurts." She didn't look at them. She needed to get it all out in the open without the distraction they provided. Because looking at them made her want to throw all caution to the wind and damn the consequences. A person could do that when it was a one-night thing or a fling. She didn't want a fling.

She wanted the forever they offered.

"But I'm a mess. You've both heard my doctors. You've both watched me struggle. We have no certainty that I'll get better—hell, I still have seizures."

"It's been seven weeks, Jazz. Cut yourself a break. It took me a year to walk normally again." Logan's tone betrayed his investment and argued against the retreat in his expression. "I know you'll do it."

"But is that fair to either of you?" She gave in to the urge and turned. They stood side by side, looking magnificent in their matching midnight blue suits. Logan's dark allure complimented Zach's golden appeal.

"You realize that you're insulting us, right?" Zach lifted his brows in challenge.

"I'm not trying to, I feel like we need to have it all out in the open. Because I want to say yes—to both of you." She'd never been so glad of a choice in her life as the one to turn around and face them when she said that. Logan straightened, his shoulders relaxed and relief flooded his expression. Zach merely smiled that singular, heart-stopping grin of his.

"We're all damaged, babe. Some scars you see and some you can't." Logan nodded to Zach. "Even pretty boy, here. You want truth—you want it all out in the open? No, I wasn't thinking about forever until I thought we might lose you. Those hours we waited to hear who in your unit had been hit were the worst in my life."

"I stared at every news report every single time word of

injuries came out of Afghanistan." Zach confessed. "I stopped counting how many times I'd get up during the night and those reports were always the first thing I checked. I marked time between your phone calls."

"Life is all the things that happen when you're not looking." Jazz licked her lips. "My mom always says that. It's a crap cliché, but I'm tired of not looking. Not when I have both of you and you better be sure, because I will personally kick your asses if you let me down."

"Logan, translate the hardass for me—was that a yes?" Zach slanted a look at his best friend.

"Sounded suspiciously like a backasswards yes. But I'm not sure."

Jazz bit her lip and laughed. "Ask me again."

"I don't know. She's threatening spousal abuse and we're not even hooked yet." Zach's blond head shook slowly. "We might want to reconsider."

Logan slapped him in the back of the head lightly. "You done reconsidering?"

"Oh yeah. Truth or dare, sweetheart?"

Laughter bubbled up through the anxiety and the worry, shoving all of the ugly little *what if* questions away. "Truth."

"Will you marry us?" Zach didn't miss a beat.

"As soon as possible." Logan tacked on, his expression fierce.

Fuck it. She only had one life. Damaged, broken into pieces and put back together again, but it was her life—and now it was theirs, too. "Yes."

She barely saw them move through her tears and then she was in Zach's and Logan's arms, sandwiched between them. Zach's mouth crushed down on hers in demanding ferocity. He released her and Logan took over. Their kisses were so different, stark with real emotion and needing, but they gave, too.

"I just want my hair back before we get married." She managed to squeeze out between kisses. The swapping back and forth made her dizzy.

"We can get you a wig." Zach's hands slid under her skirt. Her body already hummed with need for them.

"Not here." She grabbed his arm and looked to Logan. "I don't want to do this here."

"Why not, babe? We got the whole place to ourselves." Zach's fingers slid right along her labia, unerringly teasing her clit. Pleasure spiraled up from the simple caress.

"Because it's not ours. I want to go back to your home—the one the two of you made—to the room you put together for me." Stupid sentimentality maybe, but the fact that they had taken the time to set that room up for her warned her long before their words that they believed in her recovery. "I want to play in that big bed."

Logan plucked her away from Zach and his magic fingers. She bit off an oath at the withdrawal of his caresses. "Get the car. I'll blow out the candles."

"Damon's gonna kill us for wasting all this food." But Zach pivoted on a heel and raced out the door.

Logan sat her down on the chair, pushing her skirt up again and spreading her thighs. As he knelt down, he grinned up.

"Wait until we get home."

"Oh, lots of things can wait till then, but there's one little thing I wanted to taste before we moved on—" And he leaned in, breath warming her thighs, to lick up the length of her sex, tongue whirling in a thorough, hard circle of her clit.

Her eyes crossed and her mind blanked. Pleasure radiated out from his touch, and her body teased along the edge of an orgasm, but he drew back with a gentle squeeze. "Oh yeah, just as sweet as I remembered. It was killing me to look and not touch. Stay put."

He circled the room, extinguishing the candles, and she tried to retrieve the stray stands of thoughts that unraveled watching him.

Zach returned and side tossed the keys toward Logan.

"Car's out front. You're driving." He didn't slow down, scooping her up, her bare ass hanging out and all. "I get to ride in the back with Jazz."

"Hey." Logan laughed, but despite the need stretching his voice, he didn't sound angry. "That's dirty pool."

"You snooze, you lose."

Jazz held onto him as he strolled outside. The area wasn't exactly empty of people, even if Lagniappes' lights were off. That the locals were too far away to actually see her ass didn't make it any less bare. He loaded her in the car, pinching her bottom to scoot her over, and she laughed all the way as he slid into the back seat with her.

Logan muttered, climbed into the driver's seat and started the engine. "If you plan to warm her up, share the details."

"I thought we were waiting until we got home." Anticipation shot through her.

"Oh, we'll have lots to do at home." Zach echoed Logan's earlier statement, and his hand glided down her back to the zipper on the dress. In seconds it gaped around her shoulders. He tugged it forward and Jazz let it slip down her arms. Was she really getting naked with him in the back seat of the car?

Correction, she got naked. He still wore his suit.

"Are her nipples still hard?" Logan asked, in the most conversational of tones.

Zach's palm glided over one. "Affirmative. Sensitive, too."

"Hmm, is this a passive sport or can I play, too?" She pulled the dress top down and it bunched around her waist. This was a game all three could play. She climbed over, letting him brace her balance—trusting him.

"Fuck...this is gonna be a long drive." Logan sighed.

"Then go faster," Jazz tossed over her shoulder as she urged Zach's zipper down. He wasn't wearing any boxers and his cock was as hard as stone. She got wet all over again. "We need to get home now."

"Yes, ma'am."

Chapter Eleven

Zach couldn't get out fast enough after Logan slammed the car into park. The ride home involved way too much teasing. If she were one hundred percent healthy, he'd have impaled her on his cock right there in the backseat. As it was, he'd damn near come in her fingers as she caressed his dick. Logan tossed his suit coat around her and picked her up.

"I can walk."

"We know," they chorused.

"But we're moving at double time." Zach locked the car and cut around Logan to climb the stairs. He glanced over his shoulder at her soft little gasps and wasn't surprised to see his best friend's fingers tucked between her legs.

Inside the apartment, they locked up and headed for the bedroom. He stripped on the way, uncaring of where the clothes hit. He wanted to be naked with her. He'd been in a permanent state of self-denial since he'd nearly driven into her in the shower on her first day out of the hospital.

His cock strained free. He didn't slow his pace all the way to the bedside table. The low lighting gave them enough to maneuver but was better for her eyes. He found the box of condoms they'd stored in the drawer. Supplies were stocked into every bedroom, because when the time came—and they knew it would—they weren't going to let anything stop them.

Tearing open a foil packet, he rolled the condom on and sat down on the bed. Logan stood a foot away, Jazz wrapped in his arms as they kissed. Zach's heart jerked watching the slow, languorous passion and affection twining in their connection. With ball-aching slowness, Logan released her legs and she slid down his body until she stood.

Zach leaned forward and tugged the dress down the rest of the way. Somewhere between the restaurant and the bedroom, her shoes had vanished. Her panties were still in the pocket of his jacket. With shaky fingers, he peeled back the jacket and tossed it toward a chair. Logan lifted his head, and Jazz leaned back, right into Zach's waiting arms. He brought his hands up and cupped her breasts. Her nipples were swollen points.

"Do you still like having your nipples licked, baby?" He pressed a line of kisses along her ear and down the column of her throat. He pinched the hard peaks, rolling the tips with his fingers. Her long, throaty moan went straight to his cock. It sandwiched right up against her virgin ass. She was nowhere near ready to take him there. But they would have all the time in the world to play. He'd imagined how fabulous it would be to take her ass as Logan slid into her pussy, but not tonight. They'd discussed the idea several times, in person and on the phone, a fantasy they all shared. But tonight was about showing her how much they loved her.

Logan's clothes hit the floor as Zach continued the slow tease. As eager as he'd been inside the car and as tight as he was wound, he wanted to make this last for her, because as soon as he sank into her wet heat, he would blow.

"Work on her clit." Logan stepped up in front of her and leaned down to run his tongue over a nipple. Her ass clenched, the cheeks squeezing his cock, and Zach let out a hissing breath. He dropped his hands down to her thighs and began a slow, massaging rub until her legs parted. Her pussy was soaking wet from all their attention. He fingered her clit, gradually increasing the pressure. Her hands were lost in Logan's hair as he played with her breasts. Zach grew harder staring down at the flushed, plumped points.

Her ass ground against him, ramping up the pressure in his balls.

"Oh God, that feels so good." Jazz's low moans were killing him.

"It's going to get better." Logan promised. "And before he shoves that cock in you, I want another taste."

Together, they maneuvered her back onto the bed. He didn't want to stop touching her, so he turned her face to him and caught her mouth in a long kiss. Her startled gasp told him exactly when Logan settled between her thighs and went to work on her with his tongue. He leaned away from the kiss and watched the pleasure shivering in her eyes.

She nibbled along his jaw and her hands came up into his hair. He'd never let it grow, not even after leaving the Marines, but the caress of her nails against his scalp sent another pulse of want into his cock. "Hurry up." He glanced down at Logan's dark head as it moved back and forth.

Jazz stiffened and he saw the orgasm roll her under, and Logan barely rose before Zach flipped her over and positioned her on his lap. He wanted her to straddle him. She stared at him dazedly, and her flesh quivered with little quakes. She was still riding the orgasm Logan had given her. He grinned, he wanted to take his time, but that would have to wait. The minute he felt her scorching heat on the tip of his cock, she rocked her pelvis down and impaled herself.

He moaned and the sound wrapped around her own long cry. She tipped her head back and he realized that somewhere in their caresses, she'd lost her scarf. Back arching, she planted her knees and rode up then down. He braced her hips, but he couldn't pound into her the way he wanted. His cock practically wept as it was. She was so fucking tight around him, every stroke driving him closer to the edge. Her sex gripped him until his vision blacked out.

Logan caught her face in his hands and without breaking her rhythm, kissed her. They really were beautiful together. His best friend and their woman—from the moment she'd sashayed into that hotel room in Vegas, all he thought about was fucking her.

He pushed his pelvis up and met her downward shift, driving balls deep. Being that close to her made him crazy. For a year, he'd sated his hunger with his hand and thoughts of her. But she was here, recovering, and she'd promised to be theirs. He would feel her, touch her, make love to her and fuck her anytime he wanted. He was never going to let her go. She would never walk away from them again.

Above him, Logan worked her breasts and he showered her face with kisses as she strained. Her hips lost their rhythm and she cried out, her pussy clamping down on him like a silken glove. Zach's balls locked up and his orgasm detonated, ripping through him like a cannonball, and he twisted as he came.

Jazz fell forward and they both caught her. It should fuck him up to be rubbing against his best friend while they were both naked, but it felt good, right, to share this with him, like he shared so much else. All that mattered was the woman in their arms and the spasms shuddering through her with every touch of their skin.

He held her close, burying his face against hers until their breath mingled and his heart seemed to slam in time with hers.

A lazy languor rolled through Logan. He was hard as a post and ready to fuck her, but watching her and Zach gave him such immense satisfaction. The sleepy pleasure in her face, the dewy dampness on her cheeks, and the way her muscles shivered under his caresses contented him while she caught her breath. He glanced over and met Zach's eyes. They'd committed to it long before that moment, but even between the best friends, something shifted, cemented, and became more powerful. They'd always been a team, partners, and supporters.

Jazz made them whole. The soft, even sound of her breaths brought a small smile to his lips. She was asleep.

"Dude, sorry." Zach murmured.

"Let her sleep. We have the rest of our lives, and we were pretty damn hard on her." He didn't regret pushing. She needed the shove. He needed to be the one who pushed her. Gently, he scooted over and peeled her off Zach. She murmured a low sound, but Logan tucked her up against his side.

"Be right back." His best friend levered out of the bed and padded into the bathroom to clean up. The water turned on and off, but Jazz never shifted. The bed dipped as Zach returned, and he rolled onto his side, propped his head up onto his hand. "We didn't give her the ring."

"We will in the morning." By mutual consent they kept it quiet. Logan's balls ached, but he could handle a little discomfort—it didn't come close to matching the feeling of her—of all of them sharing the bed. This was why they'd invested in the king size. Why they set her up in the largest room. The room they wanted to share with her.

"We're going to need a bigger place." Zach chuckled as though following his train of thought.

"When she gets the all clear, we can talk to the Captain about those new houses he's considering building." The extension across the highway doubled the land they owned. The apartments were great for temporary visitors, but long-term staff would want more.

"Sounds like a plan." A yawn punctuated his words. "She said yes."

"I know. I was there. Get some sleep, man. I'll keep watch." He didn't have to tell the Marine twice. The man's eyes closed and the light snore an echo of their training. They knew how to sleep when needed.

Logan wasn't quite ready to yet. He wanted to lie there,

holding her, and listen to them both. Home never sounded so sweet. He cupped a hand around her breast, the pulse of her heart beating a calm cadence. Sleep came for him slowly, but he never let her go.

ॐ

Sparks lighting up his cock drove the curtain of sleep from his brain. The first weak light of morning pushed at the mini-blinds in the room. Jazz wasn't curled up next to him anymore. Zach lay with an arm across his face and sprawled over half the bed. Wet heat licked from the slit of his dick to his balls, and Logan shoved up on his elbows to look down. He went from relaxed to coiled like a spring in seconds as he watched his cock disappear between Jazz's lips. She licked him up and down, maintaining a wild, erotic rhythm. He pulsed in anticipation. She glanced up, meeting his gaze as her head bobbed up and her tongue swirled around the head.

He reached a hand down, but she shook her head slowly. "My turn to play." The words vibrated against him and sent another surge upward, spiking his pleasure. Frustration curled through him, she was all over the place, never quite lingering long enough in one motion to let him blow—and by God he was going to come. His balls sucked up tight to his body, his dick thrumming with need.

She traced her tongue across the slit again, lapping up the bead of liquid pearling there, and he growled. She laughed and opened her mouth wider, swallowing him all the way to the back of her throat. He worried she might gag, but she controlled the motion, sucking him deep. The continued torment of her tongue whirling around him was the single most sensual thing he'd ever felt. His concern burned up in a flame of need. On the next thrust, an orgasm shot through him like a bullet and he came. She never let go of him, swallowing everything he pumped out, and his heart fisted in his chest.

He slumped back against the pillows, shaking with every

tender lick she bestowed while she cleaned him. She crawled up to lay her head against his belly, and he drifted a hand down to caress her scalp, ever mindful of how tender some spots might still be.

"Fuck that's beautiful." Zach lay on his side, head propped on his hand as he stared at them. "I don't know whether to join in or ask for an encore."

Jazz laughed. "Give me a minute and I'll happily suck your cock, too."

"I love it when you talk dirty. But who gets to eat her pussy?" Zach arched a brow and Logan laughed.

"I had her for dessert. You can have it for breakfast—"

She groaned a luscious sound of anticipation. "I don't know that I'll ever walk again at this rate. I have PT in a couple of hours—" Zach shifted off the bed and her words broke off. Her body bucked, and Logan didn't have to look to know Zach found his way between her legs.

"That's more than enough time for a few more rounds, sweetheart. Don't worry, we'll feed you."

Her laughter matched his.

Yeah, this was the perfect way to start the day.

⚬

The packed and folded wheelchair leaned against the wall next to the door. Jazz sat perched on the edge of the dining room table, her robe askew and her mussed hair a testament to Logan's early morning pounce when she walked into the kitchen. He'd noticed her lack of a limp right away. He picked her up and feasted on her until the world danced. She needed another shower, but there was something almost romantic about how easily and thoroughly she came when either of her men started touching her.

She looked at the ring on her finger. She wore two of them, interlocking bands, placed there by each of the men she loved. They hadn't quite figured out the logistics of the wedding yet, but a private ceremony for the three of them would accompany whatever other splashy event they needed for their families. Families that supported the decision remarkably enough.

She'd already gotten requests for at least one boy and one girl from Logan and Zach's mothers. That embarrassing conversation left her with a quiet thrill of acceptance, too. Her own mother's response startled her, but in retrospect, it probably shouldn't have. They went out to lunch a week after Jazz said yes to the guys.

She spilled the news to her mom at a little French bistro in Southlake. Zach drove her to the date, but excused himself at her request. The late summer heat finally gave away to autumn chill in the Dallas suburb. The quiet patio, emptied of the lunchtime crowd, seemed the best place to broach the subject.

"Mom, Logan and Zach asked me to marry them and I said yes." She didn't beat around the bush with the confession. Despite the occasional twinge of worry, she committed herself to the relationship. If that meant accepting censure from others, she would take it. But she wanted her mom's approval—even if she didn't—she needed it.

"Well, I'm proud of them for waiting until you were back on your feet." Her mother cut the sandwich in half and divided the roasted fries between them. They'd split meals that way since Jazz was a child. Her mother didn't have it easy when Jazz was growing up. She hadn't been a difficult child, but she'd been heavily involved in sports, martial arts, and a fascination with her uncle who died in Beirut in 1982. Raising a Marine hadn't been easy, but her single mother was unflagging in her support.

"Mom, you get that I just said *they* asked me, right?"

Her mother seemed to take the news far better than her Episcopalian upbringing would have suggested.

"Yes, darling. I heard you. Eat your sandwich. Logan told me you haven't been eating as well as you should and that you've increased your workouts, which means a higher carb-burning threshold."

Jazz picked up the sandwich automatically, but she hesitated to take a bite. "You don't have a problem with it?"

"Do you love them?" Elizabeth Winters was a cool customer, tough, and forthright. She never minced her words.

"Yes."

"Then I think it's wonderful. They are good men, both of them. They're honorable. They love you." Wiping her fingers on a napkin, her mother pinned her with a look. "You're worried about what people think? Don't. You have served your country with distinction. You have given and given and given. You want those men. You take them. I rather like having two sons added to the family."

Jazz stared down into her coffee. Her mother's reaction and encouragement provided the last push she needed to feel totally confident about it. Parental disapproval wouldn't have changed her mind, but giving her mom the first really girly thing of her life in a wedding to plan—that was priceless.

"You planning on getting dressed today?" Zach strolled out, bare-chested and beautiful, and shook her from her musings. His jeans were open at the top button as though he'd dragged them on after crawling out of their bed.

"Yep. But I have a couple of hours before my meeting, and I didn't feel like repolishing my buttons if you guys decide to go all caveman and rip my clothes off." Her lips curled up with the tease and Zach laughed. He reached out to take her cup, and she pulled it to herself protectively. "Logan already made me spill the first cup. Get your own."

He laughed again and she loved the sound of it. "You make up your mind?"

"Yep." Logan answered for her as he wandered in, his hair still damp from the shower. The white T-shirt was a crisp contrast to his darker skin, and stretched beautifully across his muscles. "Pour me one, too."

They grabbed their mugs and joined her at the table, Zach

one-armed her right into his lap and she leaned back, almost content. Almost. After meeting with her commanding officer later in the day, the final seal would be placed on their future.

"Do I get to know what you chose?" Zach sipped his coffee, blue eyes dancing with mirth. He had to know, he'd been campaigning for her to take the offer since it arrived two weeks before.

"Recruiting. I'll be working with the local school districts and their ROTCs. I'll rotate, primarily, through Plano, Allen, and McKinney, until I'm cleared for full active and then I'll add more schools." The recruitment position was perfect. She would remain on active duty, but she wasn't stuck behind a desk. Her superior officer's offer stunned her, but both Zach and Logan supported the idea. "It's not Fallujah or Bamyan, but it's still serving."

He grinned and kissed her nose. "You're going to have the guys lining up around the block to join."

She snorted. "They can enlist, but they'll have to prove they have what it takes to be our Marines."

"As it should be." Logan grunted and tilted his chair back on two legs. He gave her a sleepy smile, but the pride and love in his expression could be mistaken for nothing else.

"So," she glanced down at the ring on her finger. "How do you guys feel about a Christmas wedding?"

~ABOUT THE AUTHOR~

Heather Long lives in Texas with her family and their menagerie of animals. As a child, Heather skipped picture books and enjoyed the Harlequin romance novels by Penny Jordan and Nora Roberts that her grandmother read to her. Heather believes that laughter is as important to life as breathing and that the Easter Bunny, the Tooth Fairy and Santa Claus are very real. In the meanwhile, she is hard at work on her next novel.

You can visit Heather at:
www.heatherlong.net

ALWAYS A MARINE

Once Her Man, Always Her Man

Can Luke and Rebecca bridge the pain of a decade long abandonment in one cold Texas night?

Tell It To The Marine

Take one Marine and introduce him to the movie star of his dreams and it sounds like a script right out of Hollywood, but for James Westwood and Lauren Kincaid, reality just might be the ticket they've both been searching for...

Proud To Serve Her

The last thing Brody or Shannon expected was a soul deep connection that brings them both wonder, but is the spark of lust enough to bring these two loners in from the cold?

Her Marine

The last thing Brody or Shannon expected was a soul deep connection that brings them both wonder, but is the spark of lust enough to bring these two loners in from the cold?